THREE FRENCH BENS

Three French Bens

Byron James-Adams

James Byron Books

Three French Bens
Copyright @ 2024 James Byron Books
www.jamesbyronbooks.com

ISBN: 978-0-9756684-2-9 (eBook)
978-0-9756684-3-6 (Paperback)

This story is fictitious. Some long-standing institutions, agencies, and public officers do exist. The characters and situations involved are wholly imaginary, and any resemblance to natural persons, living or dead, or actual events is purely coincidental.

Again a big thanks to my beta readers. Vic, Mel, Lil & M.D.M.
Cover Art: Canva by author.
Internal Book Design: Ingram Sparks.

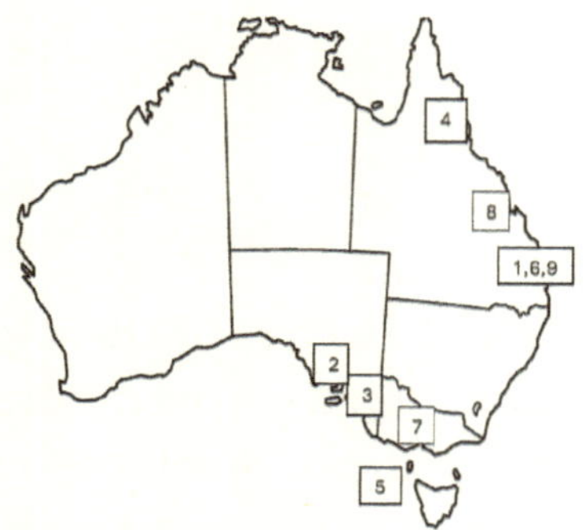

Site Locations:

1. Brisbane (Book 1) – One Tricked Phoney
2. Adelaide (Book 1)
3. Pinnaroo (Book 1)
4. Port Douglas (Book 2) – Two Hurtled Gloves
5. Corrina (Book 2)
6. Brisbane (Book 2)
7. Melbourne (Book 3) – Three French Bens
8. Rockhampton (Book 3)
9. Brisbane (Book 3)

CHAPTER 1

Rosemary Palmer was standing in the middle of a large 360° wrap-around steel counter surrounded by dead fish. 'Damn you, Nic. I reek of fish.' Rose held a bent arm to her nose, trying to spare herself from the soggy, sweet, icy smell, and was looking forward to finishing her shift within the half hour.

Fish business was slow today, yet outside, it was another sunny, hot, and humid day in Brisbane, and the throng of sounds from the Rocklea Markets wafted through the walls. The shop door opened, and Sandy, Rose's BFF, came in to collect her. 'Geez, Rose, it's a stinker out there today and, by the smell, not much better here either.'

'Very funny, Sandy. It appears that no one buys fish on these sweltering hot Brisbane days. Who knew?'

'Well, about that, tomorrow we're supposed to be heading down to Melbourne to investigate the Three French Bens Restaurant with Nic, but I may not be going. I think Dog has been catnapped. He didn't come in for his kitty dins this morning, and nothing stands in the way of our eight-kilogram Maine Coon cat and his breakfast.'

Rose tucked a recalcitrant lock of auburn hair under the hairnet and sighed. 'Did you check with Dave next door? There's a bit of catnapping going around, and lugging an eight-kilo cat like ours would at least need two people.'

'Not yet, but Dave told me that Dog has been off his food a bit. Dog won't touch anything that smells of fish, and that's all he had to feed him.'

Nic Thorn, their associate and mentor, returned from collecting a container of ice to throw down onto the open shelves to keep the fresh fish fresh and wheeled it past Sandy. 'Hey Sandy, you smell less fishy this morning. Are you still having those three showers when you return from the pre-dawn fish deliveries?'

Sandy pulled at her shirt and sniffed it. 'Yes, but it doesn't help.'

Nic tipped the ice into the open troughs. 'You know, after three weeks of doing this, I can hardly smell the dead fish, but then again, I have been walking around with my mouth agape most of the time anyway.'

Rose looked at him. 'Damn you Nic, and keep your mouth shut otherwise you'll look just like that giant cod over there.' Nic closed his mouth, smiled and held the door open so that Sandy could go back outside with him. 'Can I have a quick word, Sandy?'

'Sure. What's it about?'

'I overheard that Dog had gone missing, so I'm OK

if you're unavailable to go to Melbourne, Rose can go solo. We need to set up the apartment that we'll be staying in for the investigation, it's near Albert Park Lake on St Kilda Road. I haven't asked her yet, but the plan is that she has just returned from France, and scored a waitressing gig at the new French Bens restaurant in the New Crowd Casino. Oui Oui.'

Sandy nodded. 'OK. So, when are you going down?'

'Not for another week or so. I have to tidy a few more things up here in Brisbane with the banking fraud thing we've just finished.'

Sandy nodded. 'Dog will come back eventually.'

Rose came out of the shop, removed the little plastic hair cap, and flicked it at Nic; he caught it and folded it into his back pocket. 'What's up, why have you and Sandy gone all secret squirrel on me?'

Nic smiled. 'Nothing. It's just that we don't need Sandy down in Melbourne yet, so that means you'll be on your own. Is your French up to speed?'

'Oui, so?'

'We will be working as part of a team for a French chef, his name is Benoit Trudeau, and he's bought one-third of the Three French Bens. He's brought us in to investigate his suspicions of the numbers at the new restaurant.'

Rose nodded. 'I googled it the other day. The restaurant isn't open yet, but their website looks impressive, there were comments posted about the noise and yelling coming from the existing kitchen, interrupting the diners, that sort of thing.'

Nic smiled. 'Storm in a French teacup. Several of the existing staff are French, so they are just being all Frenchy, but that's not why we are coming in. It's the fish.'

Rose nodded again. 'Crap, or should I have said 'carp'? I wondered why I had just spent the last few weeks with my hands full of fish guts. I get the French link, but why are the fish featuring?'

'Well, this scam appears to be about mislabelling of the fish, whether it's fishy or not. Benoit noticed a discrepancy with the orders but couldn't work out how. The existing restaurant numbers are very good, and he went over them thoroughly before putting up his cash, but now he reckons there's something fishy going on.' Sandy interjected. 'Guys, enough with the fishy stuff, please. I'm getting a headache.'

Nic grinned. 'I bet I know where I could get some ice for that.'

The three of them then climbed into the car for the thirty-minute drive to Sandy's and Rose's place at West End, and Nic offered to help them look for Dog.

'So, do we bark like a dog, or call out 'here kitty, kitty, kitty, woof?'

Sandy shook her head. 'Funny, Nic, but I have an idea of what we could do. Are you guys up for early lunch?' Rose nodded and Sandy continued: 'Well, there's that new 'Chicken Take-Away' in Boundary

Street, so if we get a couple of hot chickens and spread them out on the back deck, Dog should turn up eventually.'

Rose then pulled at the front of her shirt and looked at Nic. 'Maybe I need a shower, or is something in this car smelling funky?'

Nic tapped at his jeans. 'Oh no, I'm sorry, I picked up a fillet of swordfish and have just realised it's still in my pocket. It's only wrapped in plastic.'

Rose lowered her window. 'That's disgusting. It's thirty-six degrees outside the car and fifty inside.'

'The air-conditioning is switched on.'

'Not fifty degrees. Fifty/fifty that I'll get home without being sick.' They piled out of the car, went into the chicken shop, and took turns gulping in the aroma of the roasted chickens. Nic quietly disposed of the fish fillet.

About thirty minutes later, they were home, and pieces of roasted chicken were spread across the wooden table on the back deck. Dog still hadn't returned, and they were getting concerned. Sandy had insisted they didn't start eating until the cat turned up. 'It still smells of fish out here.'

'Nope, that's me and Rose. We haven't showered yet.'

Nic excused himself, went off to have a shower and called back to them. 'I've got clean clothes here already as I've found wherever I leave my hat, that's my home. In this case, it's in an overnight bag.'

They followed him into the house and Rose started making coffee, whilst Sandy began setting up the condiments for lunch. 'Hey Rose, has Nic told you anything about the Melbourne thing yet? Act surprised when he does.'

They were about to sit down when Nic called out from the bathroom. 'Guys, I think you need to see this.'

They looked at each other and Sandy spluttered. 'Did he really just say that?'

Nic called out again. 'It's not what you're thinking, guys. So, stop thinking what you're thinking, and get in here, please.'

CHAPTER 2

Rose and Sandy made their way to the bathroom and opened the door. Nic was fully dressed, turned towards them and held out the palm of his hand; in it was a small plastic box. 'This is called an Atom Stream Cop Cam and was in the pot plant by the bath. It's a miniature spy camera.'

Nic led them back out to the rear deck, placing the tiny camera on the table. Rose picked it up and put it back down. 'Is it turned on? Will we get to see the famous Nic Thorn in the buff? The mind boggles.'

'No, there will be no boggling today, and it's not turned on. These things have a limited range and need an interface to link to. I've already called one of my guys to come in and bug-sweep the place. Have you had a party here recently?'

Rose nodded. 'You know we have. It was Sandy's thirtieth was last weekend. Sorry, but you weren't invited.'

'I'm still so disappointed about that, but who says I wasn't there?'

'Surely you didn't dress up in disguise so that you

could make an appearance. I bet you were the old geezer guzzling the free beers, getting stonkered in the corner by the fridge.'

'Nope, I just sat in the car out the front pouting, waiting for an invite. How do you think all your guests got home?'

Rose shook her head. 'What did you do? Harass all the Uber drivers until you got the driving gig?'

Nic smiled. 'I didn't need to. Every one of the drivers was one of my guys. I just made sure all your guys got home safely.'

Rose shook her head again. 'Damn you, Nic.'

Nic was about to continue when they heard someone calling out 'Yo, Nic.' Nic stood up and moved to the rear stairs. 'We're round the back, mate.' A young man ambled his way around to the backyard. 'Cripes, what's that smell? It's like...' he sniffed the air; 'Fish sticks, with roast chicken on the side.'

'That would be us. We're trying to find the cat. He's gone missing, and I thought the roast chicken might work. Have you got the toys?' The young man nodded. 'Yes, and doing a full sweep will take about twenty minutes. What am I looking for?' Nic pointed to the miniature camera.

The geek hooked up a tiny telescope to the viewfinder on his phone, inspected it from different angles, and then picked it up. 'Well, the good news is, it's not turned on. These things are fairly basic and are pretty good for fifty dollars. I would say you have an amateur here. Still do a sweep then?'

'Yep, take Rose and Sandy with you too. I don't want you going through their stuff without them.'

'Roger that.'

Rose and Sandy followed the geek back into the house, and after about ten minutes, he came out. 'I found a couple more. There is nothing in the other bathrooms or the bedrooms—just the den, kitchen, and dining room. I left them there but neutralised them so they couldn't transmit a signal. Good enough?'

'Yep, thanks, mate. I'll talk with the guys to see what's what.' The geek nodded and started to go down the stairs. 'Cripes, there's a huge fluffy animal in the way. What the hell is it?'

'That's Dog. It's their cat. He's been missing for a couple of hours. He skipped breakfast, and we were getting worried.'

'I can't even get past. Oh no, it's giving me the evil eye. I'm a dog person, and they know it. They know. I'm going out the front door if that's OK, Nic.'

Nic led him back through the house and then returned to the rear deck and Rose noticed Dog had been busying himself with the chicken pieces.

'So, how many, Nic?'

'I reckon about five or six pieces by the looks of it. Dog eats like a horse.'

Rose shook her head in dismay. 'No, not the cat versus chicken, you dope. How many cameras?'

'Just the four. I'll leave them where they are for the time being. Let's review your party from Facebook and download pictures from your phone. My geek guy has left a gizmo that can Bluetooth the pictures to the television.'

Sandy smiled. 'I'll get the popcorn, well, the popcorn chicken anyway. Oops, too late, Dog has his snout in that trough, too. He must be starving, the poor little tyke.'

They gathered around the television, and the photos began to scroll across the screen. 'Geez, you guys know some good-looking people. No wonder I wasn't invited, it would've lowered the standards.'

Rose nodded. 'Yep, that was the only reason you weren't invited. So, what are we looking for?'

Nic continued. 'Someone that you probably don't know. Someone who seems to be a little photo-shy, that sort of thing. And I'm going to throw it out there, someone left-handed.'

'Why a lefty? And how will we know anyway?'

Nic nodded. 'The woman that used Sandy's stolen ID. We have the photo of her signing fraudulent loan documents at the Community Bank Ipswich earlier this year. She was a lefty.'

Rose leaned forward. 'A bit of a leap, but who knows. Besides, how can you spot a lefty from a still picture? They might have a drink in one hand and a carrot stick in the other.' Nic shrugged. 'Don't worry. Let's keep watching to see what comes up.'

About twenty minutes into it, Nic stood up and stretched. 'This is worse than watching a five-day cricket test. I know it's only just after eleven, but I'm parched. Besides, the smell of the chicken is now wafting inside and making me hungry.' Nic headed off to the fridge. 'Are you guys OK? Wow, there is ginger cordial, ginger beer, ginger, and lime. If I didn't know any better, I'd think you like gingers – is Ed Sheeran here somewhere?'

Sandy responded. 'Don't forget Prince Harry. He's off the market now, but we keep hoping another prince will come along. ' Sandy looked at Rose. 'Or a frog. We've kissed a few so far, and none of them turned into a prince.'

They were still laughing just as Nic had returned. He sat down, pulled the top off a ginger beer, and looked at them suspiciously. 'What have I done this time?'

Sandy looked at him and chortled. 'Nothing as usual.'

He shrugged and started looking at the vision again. 'Hey, stop there. What's that?' Rose stopped the screen, and they looked at it.

'Who is she?'

'I've no idea. Let's watch where she goes and what she does.'

They kept watching the video, but it wasn't focused

on the woman, mostly on Sandy and Rose. 'Do you know who took this?'

'Dave, the next-door neighbour. He then uploaded it for us.'

'OK, that explains why he's spending so much time on you two. Boy, you guys know really, really good-looking people. Oops, sorry, that was my inner monologue speaking.'

They continued to watch for the woman, and Nic was able to manipulate the image using a joystick on the media box his geek had provided. He stopped when they saw that she had taken something from her handbag. It was a box of miniature cameras.

'OK, we know how and when, but we don't know who, or the why, and she knew her way around your place. I guess she was in your den where you had the old paper title of your home in a picture frame. She could have written down the details, then lodged the fraudulent mortgage on your house.'

Sandy nodded. 'I guess so, and she is still in the wind, isn't she? I've taken it down and blackened out the property title details.' Sandy then looked over at Rose. 'Hey Rose, did Nic let you know you are going to Melbourne alone, and we're joining you later?'

Rose shook her head. 'What's that all about, Nic? I can't set up a house in a city where I don't know anyone. How is that going to work?'

Nic smiled. 'Well, my friend Benoit will be there. I've shifted him from his place, and you are playing house together until we get there. The idea is that you and I are part of his posse, the three mouse-cat-ears and all that.'

Sandy grinned. 'So, tell us about him. Is he tall, dark, and handsome? Could he give you a run for your money?'

'Well, his surname is Trudeau, as in the Prime Minister of Canada. I guess you could Google the best-looking statesman in the world, Justin Trudeau.'

Sandy opened her phone and sighed. 'Rose, can I ask you something?'

'Sure, Sandy.'

'If I give you twenty dollars, will you teach me to speak fluent French overnight?'

Nic shook his head. 'Sorry Sandy, that won't quite work, but you'll be down soon enough. Do you want me to show you some pictures of Benoit Trudeau? I have some on my phone.'

'Really?'

'No, of course not, but we might find him on Linked-In. Benoit doesn't do Facebook.'

They pulled up the site and were disappointed because he wasn't listed. So, they googled Justin Trudeau instead, purely for research purposes. Rose diverted her gaze from the view. 'So Nic, tell me about this apartment, house, or whatever you have us slumming in?'

'They're called 'The Tyrian Apartments' at Albert Park. Do you know you're on your way around

Melbourne?' Rose continued: 'Not much, but we went down to St Kilda about two years ago for the Mercedes-Benz Fashion Week.'

'Yep, well it's on again while we are down there, and that's something else I want to talk to you both about. Do you remember Douglas and his 1955 Mercedes 300SL from the Adelaide Motor Show? Well, his little car will be in Melbourne as part of the event. He just got it valued, and it's currently one of the most valuable Mercedes in Australia. About one point eight million.'

Rose smiled. 'You sold it to him. You lost out there, didn't you?'

'Yep, that's what I do. Find stuff, lose stuff, buy stuff, and sell stuff. In this case, I stuffed up.'

'So, what do you need us for?'

'Well, you can walk, turn, and smile. Are you OK if you two are his hostesses? It means you are standing beside the car, smiling, and wearing posh frocks during the show.'

Sandy shook her head. 'Nic, we're not models, and last I read was Elle Mac and Gigi H are going to be there.'

'Sandy, yes, the elite models will be there, but Douglas trusts you both to look after him and his car. He's also in the market for a new Rolls-Royce Phantom, and you might be the ones to convince him to trade up from his Bentley.'

Sandy looked at Rose. 'Men and their cars. OK,

we'll think about it. Will we get paid as models, or will you underpay us again?'

'That's not fair. When did you last pay for anything when working with me?'

'Hey, I once bought a Tasmanian Tiger plush toy at the Hobart airport.'

'True. So, I'm going home to work on the French Bens thing, and I'll see you both at the airport to-morrow afternoon around two.'

Sandy nodded. 'Sure, but you'll have to buy your lunch as Dog has devoured all the chicken.'

CHAPTER 3

They **met at the** airport and waited for Rose's flight announcement in the QANTAS Lounge. Nic was watching an advertisement for a European holiday on the television. 'Hey Rose, there's still time to teach me French. Give me something quickly; I'll see how I go.'

'OK. If someone says, *'Voulez vous couchez avec moi ce soir,'* make sure you know how to say 'No' in French.' Nic shook his head. 'That's from a song lyric.'

Rose nodded. 'No, well, yes, it is, but it means 'Will you sleep with me tonight?''

Nic smiled. 'Err, good tip then. How do you say 'no' in French?'

'No,' and it's about the same in every language, but wave your hands around.'

QANTAS Flight QF632 to Melbourne is now boarding. Please make your way to the gate.

Nic heard the final call, and the others hadn't yet moved. 'Come on, guys. It's only going to be a week; then I'll be down there.'

Rose stood up and hugged Sandy. 'It's been a while since I've flown anywhere on my own. The last time was about ten years ago when I married my ex, Michael, and we were standing here in this airport. I told him the marriage was a sham and said I didn't even like him. He went off in a huff straight back to his parents, so I flew to New Zealand alone, and then Sandy joined me a day later.'

Nic nodded. 'That was ten years ago, Rose. I've never been that close myself. I was almost engaged once, but she walked away before we got too far down the muddled marriage motorway. Yep, it hurts, but please don't let it rule you. Life is too short to be muddled by the memory of misery.'

Rose smiled. 'Wow, that was a nice alliteration.'

'Thanks, I read it on the back of a door once. It was a big door.'

Rose gave them a wave, and they watched her walk down the gangway to board the plane. Sandy kept watching. 'I bet she won't look back.'

'Make it a twenty, and you're on.'

Rose didn't look back, and Sandy took the twenty dollars from Nic. 'Thanks for all this, Nic. We've both been a little lost since we shut down 'The She Shed,' then you came along in your shiny white Mustang and scooped us up.'

'Yep, you guys keep it real for me. I found I was sometimes losing myself in all these scams and frauds. Too many secrets get to you after a while. The day the Vita Brevis dating site hooked me up with Rose was a godsend. Then I met you, and it's been interesting so far. Rose will be OK; she is stronger than she thinks.'

Sandy smiled. 'Do you need me to do anything for the next week or so? If not, I will look into getting some more work for staging display homes and stuff. I'd like to set up a few meetings to keep me busy.'

'Nope, all good. You have my number if needed, and be careful. If something or someone doesn't feel right, walk away. It may be worth calling me if you line up any meetings so I can do a background check for you. Nic Thorn and Associates would certainly consider a merger with 'The She Shed' to open up another source of income.'

Sandy nodded. 'If you don't hear from me, I'll see you in Melbourne in about a week. And yes, we'll do the Mercedes-Benz modelling thing, but we'll need to buy some clothes for the event - look out Chapel Street, Prahran; Rose and Sandy are coming to town, and our Business Credit Cards don't have a spending limit.'

Nic shook his head, smiling. 'But they're my Business Credit Cards. You still don't have yours back from when it was stolen nearly ten months ago.'

Sandy smiled. 'I know that. I never liked living on credit anyway.'

They left the airport foyer and headed to the car-park to get the car.

A week later, Sandy was standing in Nic's kitchen at his South Bank apartment, and as Nic was leaving to collect the lunch, he called back to her. 'Please don't lie on my couch. I don't want you falling asleep on it again.'

After Nic had left, Sandy went over to the couch, sat down momentarily, and then stood up quickly and stared at it. Fortunately, her phone rang to distract her. It was Rose calling from Melbourne.

Sandy put the call on speaker whilst setting the table, and the conversation eventually led to Nic just as he was walking in the door. 'Yo, Rose. How's life in the Melbourne metropolis and co-habitation with the really, really good-looking Benoit Trudeau?

'That's why I am calling, as he hasn't turned up yet.'

'What? At the apartment or the restaurant?'

'Both. He was at the restaurant recently, but that was a few weeks ago. I went there today to do the 'bonjour' thing, and they haven't seen him either.'

'OK, did you meet the other two Bens then? Ben Patterson and François Benson?'

'Nope, I did meet three other Bens in the Casino bar. Ben Down, Ben Dover, and Ben D'Elbow, and they were happy to help me look for him.' Nic and Sandy laughed. 'Seriously, how long had you been working on that?'

'Hey, that's not fair. They were real men, eating quiche and everything.'

Nic shook his head at the comment. 'Anyway, did you meet the other Bens?'

'I met Ben P, but Monsieur Benson is missing too.

The other waitress, Amelie, told me that she hadn't seen both Ben and François in the restaurant for weeks. She told me they are avoiding each other for some reason.'

'OK, I'll make a call to Benoit to see if I can get him. If not, maybe I'll send someone around to his place to see if he's home. Give me about an hour. Unless his phone is turned off, I should be able to find him.'

'Will do. Call me when you know, and tell Sandy not to lie on the couch, or she'll go to sleep.'

About three hours later, Nic called Rose back. 'Nope. I couldn't get him, and one of my guys went to Benoit's place, and he wasn't there either. That's the bad news, Rose; the good news is that I've booked myself on the red-eye tomorrow morning. I will be there early tomorrow morning.'

'So how is that good news? I've spent a week getting this apartment all decked out and girly, and you'll storm in demanding I put all the doilies, potpourri, and frilly cushions away.'

'Rose, just what have you been doing?'

'Well, you know, a bit of this and that. Besides, I'm not a doily, frilly cushions and potpourri sort of girl, but it has been nice to spend some time alone.'

'OK, I think. I'll arrange for a driver to pick me up. Would you like me to get him to collect you along the way? Then we'll swing past Benoit's place to see what's up.'

'Sounds like a plan. I've been using the mornings

to get my sleep in sync with the late nights I'll be working.'

'Anything else?'

'Yes, as Sandy and I are now models, we don't get out of bed for less than ten thousand dollars, but I'll make an exception in your case.'

'Thanks again, I guess. As you'll be looking after an old gentleman and an old gentleman's car at the show, that's worth at least a few dollars. Two dollars, at least.'

'How is Sandy? I hope she hasn't been sitting on your comfy couch?'

'She's good, but I think she has fallen asleep whilst we were on the phone.'

'OK, wake up Sleeping Beauty, but please don't do the Prince Charming thing, as she might never wake up. I'll see you in Melbourne Airport with the driver.'

It was 7 a.m. when Rose's phone chirped as the car arrived. Rose exited the foyer and smiled at the car - it was a red, white, and blue Citroen C5, with Two Eiffel Towers and 'Three French Bens' across the panels. The driver dressed as a caricature of a Frenchman - black trousers, a horizontal blue and white striped shirt, and even the flat black beret. It was decidedly unflattering for the large man. 'Bonjour, Miss Panda-Eyes. My number is Mortie, and I'll be a driving vu to da aeroport.'

Rose looked at him and smiled. 'So, Mortie. Do you know all about my pirouettes through the waterfall at the Gallery of Modern Art in Brisbane a couple of months ago, too? Are you another one of Nic's guys?'

The driver's accent slipped back into that of a Melbourne dialect. 'No luv, I don't know anything about that, and it's my first time driving for the man. The text said my pickup was for a Miss Panda-Eyes.'

Rose climbed in beside him and they headed to the airport. 'Well, my name is Rose Palmer, not Miss Panda-Eyes, and I work with Nic. We're checking into something fishy going on down here. Have you worked with Nic before?'

'Nup luv, but my brother drives for him in Adelaide. He told me about two gals he'd driven around with Nic a few months ago. He had a hoot with them, something about the Adelaide Motor Show and selling Ex-USA Army Hummers.'

'Yes, that was me and my friend Sandy. It was the first time we worked with Nic.'

'Wow, and yep, Driver said you guys were like the best team. He's been working with Nic for a while, but it was the first time he saw him having a good time with what he does. It can be dangerous. You know that, don't you?'

'Yes, we've been lucky so far. Sandy had to Taser someone in Brisbane recently, and I had to hit someone over the head with a laptop, but that worked out all right. What do I call you then?'

'Driver too.'

'That's silly. It can't be your name.'

'Yep, and our folks were Mr and Mrs Driver. Bless them.'

'OK, I'll call you Driver Two. Let's leave it at that.'

They arrived at the airport and headed to the allocated limousine collection area. 'That's Nic, with the chinos, blue blazer, and luggage with 'Three French Bens' stickers.' Driver Two stopped the car, stepped out, and introduced himself to Nic. 'Welcome, Mister Thorn. I am Ro....'

'No, Driver...no names; family protection and safety first.'

'Sorry, um, Mister Thorn. It's my first time doing this.' Nic nodded, shook his hand and the driver continued: 'Oh, and Rose says to call me Driver Two. I'm looking forward to working for you.'

'OK, Driver Two. It's Nic, and by the way, you work with me, not for me.'

Rose got out of the car and hugged Nic. 'Thanks for coming down so quickly - there's something fishy going on at Three French Bens, and it's a bit of a worry.'

They climbed back in the car. Rose and Nic sat in the back.

'So, where to then, Mister Nic?'

'Head for St Kilda. I'll let you know once we get closer.'

They motored along St Kilda Road, down past The Esperance Hotel, and along the Esplanade. 'I think it's coming up on the left, mate. Please slow down and take a left, then we follow the road around, then take another left into Dickens Street.' Driver Two followed the instructions, and Nic added. 'Just stop anywhere.'

Driver Two found a park, and they went to get out of the car, Nic leaned over to Rose. 'Can you stay in the car? I don't know what we're going to find. Hopefully, it will be Benoit. Driver Two, and I will get this and send you a message if it's all OK. Sit in the driver's seat, with the keys in the ignition, but the doors locked.'

Rose swapped seats and nodded. 'Please be careful.'

Nic and Driver Two went further up the road, and Rose watched them ascend the steps to the front door of the single-fronted workman's cottage. Nic reached into his pocket, pulled out a set of keys and cautiously inserted a key into the lock, and they disappeared inside, closing the door behind them.

A few minutes later, Rose received an SMS, '*All clear. Lock car. Come in slowly,*' and as instructed, made her way to the property. Rose announced; 'It's me. I am coming in,' and as the door was unlocked, she slowly opened it and stepped inside. The place was a mess. Papers and smashed furniture were strewn around the room. In the middle of the floor was a square, pale rug, and in the middle was a dark red stain. Nic and Driver Two were standing on the edge of the carpet.

'It's blood, Rose. I have tested it.'

'Do you know whose it is?'

'Nope.'

'Do we call the Police?'

'Not just yet, as we don't know what this is. It could be related to Benoit Trudeau being missing, or it might just be that someone has robbed the place. It looks like they were interrupted, though, as the mess is only in this room. Maybe Benoit came home, saw the mess, got worried, and left. It's still a break-in, even if you have the key.'

'Whose place is this? Is it Benoit's?'

'Nope, it's not his, but he's been living here for a few months. It's one of the places that I have access to. I thought it was too small for the four of us, so I booked the apartment at The Tyrian.'

'What do we do now?'

'Let's look around, but first, let's all go back to the front door and put rubber bands over our shoes; that way, it makes it easier for the Police can track our movements on the carpet. The timber floors are harder to take prints from, but not so from the rug. After all that, we may call the Police.'

The three of them went to the door and put the rubber bands on their shoes. Rose was wearing flats, and Nic had a pair of Florsheim loafers. However, Driver Two had Blundstone ankle boots on and kept snapping his band, trying to put them on.

He gave up and decided to keep watch from outside. 'I'll stay here and keep a lookout.'

Rose and Nic re-entered and went directly to the blood stain. Nic carefully re-traced his steps on the carpet when he had taken the swab for the test. Rose was watching him. 'What are we looking for?'

'Something that doesn't fit. If Benoit was kidnapped, he might have left a clue, something subtle. If he wasn't, it could be anything. He told me he'd discovered some things after the partnership buy-in, but unfortunately, he'd already handed over the money. Don't touch the papers on the floor. We'll try to separate them with a plastic ruler or a kitchen knife. I'll see what I can find.'

Nic collected a couple of plastic rulers from the office. They scoured the lounge room and decided there was nothing of interest scattered amongst the debris. Rose looked over to the other side of the room. 'I'm sorry, Nic, I have to, you know, spend a penny. I should've gone before I left the apartment. Will it be OK if I use the facilities? We might have to explain it to the Police, though.'

'Yep, down the hall, first door on the left. All good, and it's rare that someone breaks into a house and uses the bathroom anyway.' Nic watched as Rose made her way carefully down the hall. She was crab-walking sideways with her back against the wall.

Driver Two called out from the front door. 'Yo, my man Nic, you need to hear this. Mrs Brosnan from next door says she saw Benoit about a week ago but nothing since.'

Nic greeted the elderly neighbour, confident no one else was in the house. Mrs Brosnan began: 'Hello,

Mister Thorn. I haven't seen you for a while, dear. I heard that you were living in Brisbane and.....' the woman was craning her neck to see around him, so Nic closed the door behind him. 'Sorry, Mrs Brosnan, it's a bit of a mess in there, and it looks like we may have been robbed. Did you happen to see something?'

'Oh, sorry, dear, your friend Mr Trudeau was here about a week ago. He came in with another man, and I think he was French too, as they kept talking loudly and all Frenchy. I picked up a couple of words: poisson is fish, and argent is money. I love watching that French chef, Manu Fiedel, on the telly.'

'That's good, Mrs Brosnan, thanks. My friend Rose speaks French, so I'll check with her when she returns, but please go back home and keep your doors locked, just in case. If anybody comes back, please give me a call.'

Nic and Driver Two were at the front door watching Mrs Brosnan going home when they heard Rose calling from the bathroom. 'I can't get the tap turned off, and it's getting all hot and steamy in here. The top of the cold water tap is missing, so I had to use the hot water, but now I can't get the damn thing shut off.'

'OK. Are you all right in there, decent and everything?' Nic went inside, rapped on the bathroom door, and waited for Rose to open it. 'Yes, just get in here. I don't want to open the door and let all the steam out. The fan isn't working either, and there's no window. Who builds a bathroom without a window?'

'Well, I didn't build the house, but I organised the renovations. Maybe it needed a woman's touch, and you weren't around. Open the door, and let me in.'

Rose opened the door, and a plume of steam spilled into the hall. The bathroom was still very hot and steamy. Nic stepped over to the sink, and Rose moved out of the way. 'If this is your place, does it have any cameras as you have in your Brisbane apartment?' Nic smiled. 'Nope, I didn't think they were necessary. Besides that, where's the top of the cold tap?'

Rose grimaced. 'No idea. I just turned the hot tap on and can't get it turned off. Stop yelling at me.'

'OK. I'll just go outside and turn the water off at the mains.' Nic moved quickly back to the front door, down the front path, pulled up the water panel lid and turned the lever. 'The water's off.' He made his way up the path and was stopped by Driver Two at the front door.

'This wasn't a break-in, Nic. The TV and stereo are still here, mate, and the money tin on the kitchen bench has about a hundred bucks or so in it. Old Mrs Brosnan said she stays home all day, too. Her lounge room faces the street, so she watches everyone that comes and goes.'

'Maybe Benoit and François Benson were here and argued over something.'

Rose then called out. 'Hey Nic, are you coming back? The water's off, but there is something I want to show you.'

Nic went back to the bathroom, and Rose pointed towards the bathroom mirror as there appeared to be a word smeared on the glass. It had held its form with the steam and was written with Vaseline: YodaNT

Rose looked at it. 'What's YodaNT?'

'It's from Star Wars—the little green fat-rat-looking dude with the funny way of speaking. 'Do or do not, there is no try'. That sort of thing.'

'Nope, means nothing to me. 'Star Wars' is a movie isn't it?'

'Haven't you seen any of them? The first one was made in seventy-seven.'

'Well, actually, no, I was born in ninety-one.'

'Rose, they have made about eight more since then.'

Driver Two called from the front door. 'You guys right in there?'

'Yep, but did you see any Star Wars merchandise around here? For some reason, 'Yoda' is written on the mirror. I think he wants me to look for it. It has my initials next to the word.'

Driver Two continued. 'I have to admit I was having a bit of a gander at his bedroom. Your French dude has a display cupboard full of those toys. I sort of jiggled the lock a bit, and it sprung open. I may have broken it, mate, sorry.'

'All good, but it must mean something.'

Rose nodded. 'Nothing means nothing unless it means something, doesn't it?'

'So true, Rose. To the rat cave then.'

Nic and Rose moved across the hall and into Benoit's bedroom. It was styled decidedly French. The Eiffel Tower and Arc de Triomphe photos on the walls, and an Audrey Tautou movie poster from the 2001 film 'Amelie'. Nic saw the display cabinet; pride of place was the latex model of a metre-high Master Yoda holding a lightsabre. The large, round sword was glowing. Rose moved to take a closer look. 'Cripes, is that a doll? Who collects this stuff? Grown men?'

'Yep, and this little critter in mint condition is worth about a hundred and fifty dollars. The one you need to get your hands on is life-sized. They're about six grand's worth.'

Rose sighed. 'I once had a Barbie doll collection, but my brother used it as target practice with his slingshot. I was about ten at the time. It put me off collecting things for life.'

Nic opened the cabinet, carefully extracted the Yoda model, and put it on the cupboard. 'You won't want to look at this. I may have to disrobe this little guy, and it might not have any underwear.' Rose began to turn around, and Nic laughed. 'Damn you, Nic. What are you looking for?'

Nic searched the model, then picked it up and shook it. There was a rattle within the model, so he snapped it off from the base. 'This.' He opened his hand to show her it was a Yoda-styled thumb drive.

Driver Two was now standing at the bedroom door

and saw Nic's discovery. 'I didn't see a computer here, so maybe something was taken after all.'

Nic nodded. 'Yep, or maybe Benoit just took it with him. We don't know yet what the blood stain is all about either.'

The three of them returned to the car, and Mrs Brosnan gave them a wave from inside her front parlour. Nic hesitated just as the others climbed in. 'Excuse me whilst I make a call as I need to get the house tidied up and arrange a plumber. We need to get this thumb drive looked at, too.' Nic made the call and climbed into the back seat with Rose. 'Where to, Nic?'

'West Brunswick. I have a computer guy that can look at this for us. It must mean something. Otherwise, I wouldn't have had to break the Yoda model to find it.'

CHAPTER 4

They drove back through the city via the Victoria Markets and onto Nic's computer geek's place. Driver Two stopped the car, and Nic stepped out. 'Please stay here. This guy used to work with me years ago but he turned on me for some reason. I know he's the best at what he does, so I keep using him.' Nic went to the front gate and pressed the intercom. It was answered immediately: 'Nic Thorn, you son of a nun.... What do you want this time? I haven't got your money.'

'I need your help, Chewy. I have a thumb drive to look at. I don't know what's on it, but it could be important. Oh, and can my friends come in too?'

'Sure, so you reckon you still need protection from me and my dragons.'

Driver Two and Rose stepped out of the car, and a voice boomed from a loudspeaker attached to the undercroft of the house. 'The pretty lady with the big brown eyes can come in, but the big French dude has to stay with the car.'

Nic nodded that he was good with that, then turned to Driver Two and motioned to him to keep an eye on things. They slowly and carefully moved towards the house, and when Rose tried to take Nic's hand just as the front gate clicked open. He softly brushed it away. The geek stepped out from the stoop, went up to Nic, sized him up, hugged him and then slapped each other's backs. 'Who's the stunner then? You always said, 'Don't with women, animals and children,' yet here you are with this one.'

'Well, this is Rose. She urgently needed a '+ 1' for a funeral, so I turned up and swept her off her feet with my broomstick.'

'No, he didn't, Mr....'

'Call me Chewy, you know from 'Star Wars'? Chewbacca.' The two men then made the guttural Wookie sound in unison.

Rose looked at them. 'What the hell was that?'

Nic smiled at his friend. 'Chewy, she doesn't know Star Wars, but reckon I can still convert her.' Chewy looked over, shaking his head. 'Not a 'Trekkie' either?'

Rose shook her head. 'Nope, sorry, Mr Chewy. I don't have much idea what that is. I don't go to the movies much, but Nic tells me the cute little films might be worth seeing, eventually.'

The men both shook their heads with mock dismay and Chewy then led them inside. The rooms were immaculate, with modern furniture, sparse but stylish. They made their way to the kitchen area, and Chewy pushed a button on the wall. A double door, recessed in the wooden floor, parted, and a handrail rose from the floor. 'Down we go, down into the dungeon. The dragons have gone for a walk, so we'll be safe down here, Rose.'

Rose shrugged and Nic noticed. 'Nope, mate. Rose doesn't know about 'Dungeons and Dragons' either.'

Chewy looked at her. 'My God, where have you been?'

Rose shrugged again, and they stepped down into the void. At the last step, the space revealed itself as a complete computer studio, with the entire house sitting above wall-to-wall screens and about ten different types of computers, each showing different views. There were seven mobile phones on a table, various laptops, and wires going everywhere. There was also a TV screen in a vertical position showing a flying saucer on the screen, with the words 'The Truth is Out There' scrolling along the bottom of it.

'Impressive basement, hey, Rose?'

'Yes, but I don't know what it all means or what you geeks spend all your time on. It must make for an interesting electricity bill every quarter.'

'Solar baby, I don't pay a thing. Anyway, Nic, what have you got?'

Nic handed him the thumb drive, and Chewy plugged it into the nearest laptop. 'I'll download it first, and then we will open from there, not directly from the drive.' The computer did its thing, and Chewy clicked on the command to extract the drive. 'Oh, that's not good, Nic. The drive has an auto-deletion program. We might only have one chance to download it.'

'Be careful mate; it might be evidence too'.

'Oh, thanks for the tip. Did you nick it, then... Nic?'

'Funny mate, and no, it was at my place at St Kilda. Benoit had it hidden inside his Yoda.'

'Man, you didn't snap it off to get it out, did you? The models have a click mechanism to take them off the base. You'll owe the Frenchman for that; he might go Jabba the Hut on you.'

Rose moved up to them. 'Is there anything on it?'

Chewy nodded. 'Could be, but I'm just running a second virus scan before I do anything, Miss Panda-Eyes from the Gallery of Modern Art in Brisbane.'

'You know about that too?'

'I know about it. I uploaded it to the net after Nic sent it to me. But don't worry, as everyone who has downloaded since has left a tracking trail. I've attached a worm so we can watch them when they are watching you if we need to. Some of their virus scanners pick it up, but mostly they don't. I put it with a WORD.doc file, clever, hey?'

'You lost me at 'uploaded it'. I don't do computer speak either, sorry.'

'Nic, just what do you get from your new associates then? ...Sandy and Rose, Ah, I understand; they're your foils. Brilliant, just brilliant. Whilst you're doing your thing over here, Sandy and Rose are doing their thing over there, and no one is watching you.' Chewy smiled at his conclusion, then continued. 'So, what's brought you to be sunny, wet, cold and hot Melbourne this time?'

Rose looked at him. 'That was the four seasons in one day, Chewy.'

'Yes, courtesy of Neil Finn and Crowded House. Great band, great song.'

'Sorry, Chewy, I'm not much of a music person either. I've seen Nic play the guitar, though; he's pretty good.'

'I know. He's not up to my standard, but can hold his own. I've been working with Nic for about ten years. We started to put this show together after we met at Uni in Brisbane. I came back here after that to set all this up. We'd known each other from back in the Mildura days. Has he told you the story about my lemon tree?'

'Yes, but I promised him never to mention it again. Do you know his twin sister?'

Nic interjected. 'Rose.'

'Yes, Nic?'

'You promised you wouldn't go there. Protection of family and all that.'

'Can't stop a girl from trying, can you?'

'Hey, Nic.' Chewy nodded towards a C.C.T.V. vision of the front streetscape; 'Why did you tell your driver guy to leave? The car has just left.'

'I didn't. I'll call him and see what's going on. Can I

make a call from down here? You haven't got a jammer in there, have you?'

'Can do. I'll turn it off, and whilst you're doing that, I'll work on downloading this thumb drive.'

Nic stood up and waited for Driver Two to answer his call, and fortunately, he did even though he was driving. 'Hiya Nic, what's up?'

'Where are you, and what's going on? I thought you were going to wait for us out the front?'

'I was, but then two dudes came up to me. They told me they knew where Benoit was, so I'm following them back to wherever.'

'Not a good idea. How did they know we were looking for him? And besides, how do you know they are legit?'

'I guess I didn't. I thought you might like me to look while doing your stuff there.'

'Nope, sorry, it doesn't work that way when you work with me. I make the decision; then we make the decisions. There is no '*you*' making decisions. It might make for a difficult conversation with your brother if something happened to you on my watch. Where are you?'

'Sorry, mate. I'm just coming up towards the zoo. I am new at this stuff. I just thought.....'

'OK, turn around when you can and come back here. If they follow or stop you, tell them we finished early and are coming out. Other than that, we'll have to swap the car over.'

'Have you finished in there then?'

'Nope, but that's not the point. Hit the intercom when you get here, and we'll come out with a bug sweeper in case they are trying that on, too.'

'OK. Roger that, and sorry again.'

About thirty minutes later, the buzzer went off in the computer basement, so they met with Driver Two. Chewy did a bug-sweep of the car and discovered a device attached to the underside of the wheel arch. He carefully extracted it and handed it to Nic. 'Wow, top shelf stuff, this one. These guys aren't the ones to mess with. You are looking at a couple of hundred dollars for this. It's called a Live Drive Tracker. Who are these guys?'

'Don't know yet, Chewy.'

The group then went back inside and back down to the basement. Chewy brought up the information downloaded from the thumb drive, extracted various folders, and displayed them over four computer screens. 'Nothing much here, Nic, just the previous financial reports of the business; a Purchase Contract and a Partnership Agreement. It looks like they changed the business's names when Benoit Trudeau bought in. It was French then but was previously called 'Les Deux'. I remember when it used to be an up-market Italian restaurant, and now it's going French. I haven't been to the New Crowd Casino for ages, not my scene. I can do some more digging if you like.'

'Yep, keep working on it. I don't know if Rose and

I will be starting this week if Benoit doesn't turn up anyway. There must be something here. Oh, is it rubbish collection day today? Has the rubbish bin been emptied as yet?'

'Nope, they come around lunchtime these days. Why?'

'Well, the car tracker you found might just get thrown into a rubbish bin.'

Nic went outside, dropped the Tracker in the kerbside bin, then they left Chewy's place and headed off to change the car over. Driver Two approached Nic. 'Sorry again, Nic, but what about all these car stickers? They cost a couple of hundred bucks. Am I chucking them in the bin too?'

'Nope, We'll peel them off and leave them with Benoit. We have to change this car over though. Head for Port Melbourne, where the depot is.'

'Roger that. Do you think those dudes are going to come after us?'

Rose intercepted. 'Nope, Driver Two, we don't know what we know until it's known.'

'Rose.'

'Yes, Nic?'

'You sound more like me every day, and it makes me sound crazy.'

CHAPTER 5

Nic met with his car people and they did an exchange. They were now driving another Peugeot; it was white and looked like everything else on the road. 'Tell me about the two guys that came up to you then.'

'Well, one was tall and thin. I copped a whiff of burnt garlic or something like that from him. I guessed him to be an Aussie, maybe of a European background; he had large hands and a bandage on one finger in his late thirties. Didn't have a wedding ring on.' Driver Two thought a bit more and continued. 'The other was shorter and fatter. I reckon he is in his early forties. Wore a red bandana around his face, over his nose, not on his head. Both of them had dark black hair. The tall guy was the only one that spoke to me. They didn't say much but told me they knew where Benoit was. I took them for true blue. Sorry, Nic, it sounds so stupid now. Oh, and they were driving a blue Hyundai Elantra. I didn't get car registration details.'

Rose looked at him. 'How long did you see them? Half an hour then?'

'Nope. I would say about three minutes, including the talking.'

'Great job, mate, so we know....' Nic's phone rang, and he held up his finger to stop the others from talking. 'Hi, Mrs Brosnan. How can I help you? .....Okay, that's interesting, and no, my guys won't be there yet as they are due tomorrow. Can you describe them to me? Keep yourself safe.' Nic listened to the narrative and then disconnected. 'Sorry guys, lunch might have to wait. We're heading back to St Kilda now. It looks like our two friends, let's call them 'Lofty and Lardy', maybe back at the house.'

Driver Two drove to St Kilda, went up Dickens Street and slowed the car to a crawl. 'That looks like it could be the car.'

Nic nodded. 'OK, this time I'm calling the Police. Stop here, and I'll jump out. I can go around the back of Mrs Brosnan's place and get into mine through her garage.'

Rose gave him a look of concern as Nic climbed out of the car and he continued: 'Guys, give me ten minutes. Drive up to the front, stay in the car, and keep the doors locked.'

They watched Nic move down the street; he hurdled the picket fence next to Mrs Brosnan's and made his way between the two properties. Driver Two looked at Rose in the rear vision mirror. 'How long have you been doing this stuff with Nic? You guys seem like a really good team.'

'About ten months. I needed a +1 for a funeral in Brisbane, and Nic turned up in a white Mustang and an Armani suit. Who does that? Then I introduced him to my best friend Sandy, and our lives got a little more exciting. We like it; it makes us feel like we are doing something worthwhile and shines the light on the dodgy stuff that goes on in this crazy world around us.'

'So, what about romance? That sort of thing? He's one good-looking dude.'

'Nope, he is purely professional. We know it can be dangerous sometimes, but everything is well-coordinated. He makes sure we feel safe, and we know that we can walk away if we don't.'

Rose was about to continue when her phone chirped with a message from Nic: *'Not them. Police here. Stop talking about me.'* Rose held it up so Driver Two could see it, and then they stepped from the car and went to the front gate.

Mrs Brosnan and the Police were there and were deep in conversation. Nic took the lead. 'Sorry, Officers, it's all a misunderstanding. It's my place, and the guys Mrs Brosnan spotted were here to clean up after a party. They were supposed to be here tomorrow but didn't tell me they were coming early.' The Officers took a couple of notes and moved away.

Driver Two nodded towards the car. 'Sorry, Nic, I thought it was the car. It could be the same, but I haven't seen the dudes Lofty and Lardy lurking around.' Nic nodded. 'Don't worry about it. You've passed every test I could throw at you so far. It's great that you and your brother both give the same consideration for vigilance and our safety. Thanks for that.' Nic then approached Mrs Brosnan, guided her back into her house, and gave her a peck on the cheek when she opened her front door.

The three of them bade her farewell and returned to the home. It was spotless; the red-stained rug had been removed, and all the papers were collected. The damaged furniture had been substituted like for like, and Rose noticed the broken Yoda doll had even been changed over. The water was back on, and the bathroom taps had been replaced. 'Geez, your guys are good. They were here about half an hour?' Nic smiled. 'No, it took them forty-five minutes, I think. That's what Mrs Brosnan said anyway.'

Driver Two looked towards the car across the road. 'Can we take a little look-see anyway? It looks like the same car, mate.'

'Yep, let's do it.'

The two men went over the road whilst Rose stayed in the house preparing the lunch. Driver Two walked around the car. 'What do you think then? I reckon it's the same car, mate. There's a red bandanna in the back, and the stain on the back seat might be blood. Lardy might have had a cut or a bloodied nose that he needed to mop up, or it could be Benoit's.'

'Yep, let's leave it, but Chewy gave me this.' Nic

extracted a car tracker from his pocket and casually squatted down to tie his laces. Nic leaned against the back wheel as he rose and placed the appliance under the wheel arch. 'It will be interesting to see if the car is here in the morning, too. I'll get Chewy to turn the tracker on tomorrow; if they do a bug sweep tonight, it won't get picked up.'

They returned to the house, and Rose served the sandwiches for lunch. Driver Two looked over to Nic. 'You've been doing this spy stuff a while, haven't you?'

'Yep, mate and it is getting tougher. There are so many scammers out there, but I don't just do this stuff. I also buy stuff, sell stuff, find stuff, and lose stuff...I wanted to go to Sandy's thirtieth birthday party, but Rose told me to get stuffed.'

Rose looked at him, 'But you came anyway and ensured everyone got home safely. You didn't even come in to say hello.'

'That's not fair; besides, there were too many good-looking people already.' Nic laughed at his statement, and Driver Two looked at them. 'Come on, boys and girls, play nicely.'

Rose looked over to Nic. 'He has just passed test Number Three, telling us off.'

Nic continued. 'OK, we need to talk about the restaurant. I'll need to go there with or without Benoit. We'll have to assume we will start working there on Saturday night. It's the official opening on Sunday.

So, can you take me there tomorrow and set things in motion? Remember, I don't have to speak French or even be French. That's your role. I am Benoit's silent Sous Chef.'

'How is it going to work if he isn't there? And what about Monsieur Benson?'

'I don't know yet. Let's play it that we don't if they're missing, but it might not even come to that.'

They spent the remainder of the day sitting around. Rose was throwing French words at Nic to enlighten him. Driver Two had picked it up much quicker than Nic, so they started having simple conversations. Finally, Nic had had enough and stood up, then Rose realised she was about to spend the night with Nic without a chaperone. 'Err, Nic, as Sandy isn't with us yet, and Benoit is still missing. Shouldn't you stay here just in case? What if Benoit returns here and needs to play with his little Yoda doll?' Nic nodded. 'Good point, but I think we'll manage.' Nic locked the front door and Driver Two drove them to the apartment.

Rose and Nic were riding the compact elevator with an older woman and were all being pushed closer together. Nic kept smiling whilst Rose backed into him. The buxom woman had a big-brimmed fancy hat and was carrying two large suitcases. The lift chimed at their floor, they stepped out and the woman looked at Nic. 'I'm sorry, Mr Handsome. Would you mind looking for my key? It's in the pocket of my tunic.'

Nic moved forward, fumbled for the key, and the

woman started to squeak, then muttered something about sexual harassment. All the while, the trio edged closer to the apartment door. Rose gently pushed the woman out of the way, opened the door and stepped inside, closing it behind her. It was then she realised Nic was still on the other side.

There was a banging on the door, and Rose opened it to see Sandy and Nic beaming at her. 'Damn, you two, and here I thought I would be spending the night alone with Nic.'

'Nope. Sandy sent me a message that Jetstar had a cheap flight from Brisbane to Melbourne, so she jumped onto it, and here she is. It's good to see that the latex disguise still works. I don't know that we will need it in Melbourne, though.'

Sandy and Rose hugged. 'At least you don't smell of fish anymore, Sandy, just of mothballs.'

'Yes, and although this outfit suits me. I think we need to get over to Prahran to buy some clothes for the Mercedes-Benz Fashion thing, don't you?'

Rose nodded. 'We do, and we have a driver to take us there. He is the brother of Driver that we had in Adelaide, and to save confusion, we call him Driver Two.'

Sandy continued. 'But what about the restaurant thing? When is that all happening? Do I need to put the mask and old lady stuff back on? I could be useful as a food critic at the Casino or part of the local old fogies' pokies tag team.'

Nic shook his head, 'Not quite Sandy, but there is a problem. We haven't found Benoit, and Francois Benson is still missing too. Rose and I will go there on Saturday to set up things. We might have to fake it until we bake it.'

'That's clever, Nic, but seriously?'

Nic shrugged, and then his phone rang. It was Chewy. 'Yup, what you got, mate?'

'I have found what the issue is. It was in the Credit and Debtor Listings. I won't bore you with the details, but the main fish supplier is closely linked to Ben Patterson. Nothing exists until you cross-reference the suppliers to the actual fish invoices. The restaurant has been serving award-winning gourmet French fish meals, like Matelotte Normande and Bouillabaisse, using Basa, John Dory, and even lesser-grade salmon. It's no wonder Benoit is annoyed after handing over his cash. The restaurant numbers would show over-inflated profits. It was all in a subfolder named: 'Fishy Stuff'. I should've gone there first.'

'OK, thanks. That gives me an idea of what's happening, but we must find out who is behind it. Rose and I'll be heading up there tomorrow, and hopefully, Benoit and Monsieur Benson will turn up.'

Nic closed the call and then looked at Rose. 'OK, now we know what Benoit was looking into. Chewy found the link. They have been buying lesser-grade fish and presenting the meal at a higher price. There's no obligation to accurately advertise the fish they serve as it comes down to the integrity of the restaurant, the prestige of service and quality of the presentation.'

Rose nodded. 'It doesn't sound fishy at all then, does it, Nic?'

Nic shook his head. 'Stop with the fish jokes, please. Let's go to dinner. I want to try the Lord Cardigan Restaurant over at the lake. They do traditional Australian fare and don't serve fish. They serve people, just not fish.'

CHAPTER 6

They took an Uber to the restaurant, and over dinner, the conversation continued with Rose raising her concerns. 'Surely if the Australian Food Standard people find out they damage their reputation and any hope of getting a Michelin Star?'

'Not quite; the Michelin Star rating doesn't exist in Australia. They use Chef Hats.'

Sandy nodded. 'Enough of the silly, smelly stuff then. Tomorrow, Rose and I will hit the shops looking for our modelling outfits. Are you interested in a day of shopping with us?'

'Let me think... I've thought about it, and don't want to come. I need to spend more time looking for Benoit and maybe do some more investigation stuff with Chewy. I could lend you Driver Two, but he would be better with us if we need a third wheel.'

They returned to their apartment, and Sandy pointed to the kitchen. 'By the way, Nic, it's time you put that culinary expertise into practice. What are you going to dish up for breakfast?'

'Eier auf toast, followed by oeufs sur toast, then

uoca su pane tostato, huevos tostados and my best-prepared dish, cold cereal.'

'Oh, I am so egg-cited, and by the way, can you do all of that without cracking a dad yolk, please, Chef?' They headed off to their respective bedrooms for a good night's sleep.

In the morning, Nic had prepared breakfast and despite his lack of attempts to do anything other than eggs on toast in four different languages, it was mildly delicious. He was now showing them how to crack an egg one-handed, and as they couldn't quite manage it, Sandy decided to show Nic the simplest way was to drop them one-handed to the floor. They cleared the breakfast dishes, and Nic cleared the broken eggs from the floor.

It was mid-morning when Rose and Sandy caught an Uber to the boutiques of Chapel Street. 'When does the Fashion thing start? I'm getting mixed up with all the days of the week. I thought we were working long hours when we ran 'The She Shed,' but this is getting all too much.'

'You're kidding, aren't you? We have a Business Credit Card with unlimited expenses and are in the middle of one of the best shopping precincts in Australia. Do you want to step back from all of this because we're too busy?'

Sandy smiled. 'No way, I was just checking that you were listening.'

'Very funny. This Fashion show is next Wednesday

at the Melbourne Convention Centre, so let's get shopping.'

Sandy nodded. 'Nic said that Douglas is still keen for us to be there and that his Mercedes-Benz will be displayed for the first and last days. It's only four hours though, as he worries about it getting dusty. Who knew? You buy and store a car in an airless plastic bubble for safe keeping, and it makes you money.' Rose continued. 'By my reckoning, we need at least six outfits each day: one to arrive, one to wear during the show, and one to leave in. I reckon a budget of about twelve hundred each might see it. For all three, I think.'

Sandy nodded. 'So where are we going first? I know you are partial to this year's Bass & Side collection, and I don't think the other models will use local anyway.'

'Yes, but how about we give them the heads up? See if they might sponsor us for wearing their label, and we might even be able to make a little pin money for ourselves.'

They made their way down to Bass & Side at No. 400 and were ready to launch into the pitch to the staff, but fortunately, the National Sales Manager was at the store when they arrived, and they knew her from when they had their boutique in Brisbane: 'So, ladies, are you after three outfits each? I'm sure we can accommodate that. I know it's a bit to ask, but as you will be wearing our couture, we are not expecting it to be returned. Would you be happy to keep the outfits instead of us paying the standard $1,000 per day each? Are you OK with, say, $500?' Rose and Sandy couldn't nod quickly enough.

'Oh, and sorry, which Modelling Agency are you from again? I know that you don't have your Brisbane fashion store anymore. Are you just doing Car Shows and Runways to make ends meet?'

Rose hesitated. 'We aren't with a fashion agency. We're only working on-site during the Fashion Show looking after a car. Sorry if we misled you.'

'Oh, that might make a difference. I might have to rethink my offer. Which site is it then?'

Sandy responded. 'We're guarding a Mercedes 300SL. We know the owner. He wants us to look after him and his little car.'

'Right, so.... wow, you two have got that gig. Every television station will be on the car, even the international ones. I'll make fifteen hundred dollars each for you then. This is going to be big for us. Please excuse me as I have to call my Company Directors to let them know.'

Sandy looked at Rose. 'Have we done the right thing, Rose? Are we allowed to represent a local Fashion Company at the show?'

Rose shrugged. 'I guess so, but I don't know if we were supposed to keep it on the down-low, Nic's secret stuff and all that, but he did suggest it in the first place.'

After about three hours of trying thirty different outfits each, they were exhausted and called Nic to see if Driver Two could come and collect them. Nic was eager to hear of their purchases. 'So, Sandy. How was Chapel Street, and did my Business Credit Card get a battering?'

'Actually no, but we did settle on four outfits each, and they'll be delivered to the apartment on Tuesday afternoon for the show on Wednesday. We only managed to visit one fashion outlet. Do you think we can come back on the weekend to do some real shopping?'

'Err, haven't you spent all day in Chapel Street?'

'Yes, but that was for work.'

CHAPTER 7

They had spent the morning at Chewy's place going over his findings. Chewy was reviewing his notes: 'The further I went into the information, the more I realised that Ben Patterson was the key. Benoit had managed to find more links between the fish suppliers and falsified invoices. There were even browser links that went off to websites. I was able to access the website and found more anomalies. This Benoit guy is very thorough. I feel sorry for him and hope we can sort this out.'

'Yep, and find him too.'

Chewy continued: 'OK, overnight, I managed to triangulate the last known use of his phone. It didn't turn out to be much of a lead though, as it was near your place off Dickens Street.'

Driver Two looked over at Nic. 'It might be something, though, as we think their car was in the street. Did you have the tracker on?'

Chewy responded. 'Yes, but I don't think the car has moved, that may mean it's been dumped.'

Rose chipped in. 'Not really, Chewy, as it might also

mean they live in the area and haven't used the car yet.' Sandy interjected. 'Nothing means nothing until it means something. Has anyone been back there since to see if the car has been moved or that the tracker fell off?'

Driver Two looked at Nic. 'Geez, these guys are good, aren't they? They aren't trained in the fine art of what you do, but it's great to work with such a tight team. All thinking differently, but the same. Shall we drive over there and have a look?'

Chewy stood up and stretched. 'Nope. I'll get a drone to do it. It'll take about a minute to get it organised rather than the thirty minutes to drive over.'

Chewy sat back down, slid his wheeled stool over to another keyboard, turned on the screen, and immediately, a picture appeared. It was a live stream from across the top of an office building. He plugged in a console with two joysticks, pulled the lanyard strap over his head, and pushed on the throttles, and the drone started to rise. 'The drone is down the road from your place. It's on top of the Victorian Water-ski Association's building. They have them on their roof for anyone to use once you sign a damage waiver.'

The group watched as he skilfully piloted the drone towards Nic's house, following the streets for guidance, and soon, was hovering over the top. They could now see the car in the vision. 'Well, the car has moved as it's now further up the road, so we need to go there. Maybe we could go door-knocking to see who owns it.'

Nic nodded. 'Yep do that, but Rose and I must go to the restaurant. Do you think you guys could handle it? I don't want any risks taken. Maybe if one of you stays in the car with the Police on the quick dial. I reckon we use the 'lost dog' ploy. Sandy, it might be worth putting the 'old lady' disguise back on since you brought it, but you'll have to avoid my place as Mrs Brosnan might be on the lookout.'

Chewy nodded. 'We are up to it, Nic, so don't worry. It's the first time I'll be out on the field. Whoo Hoo.'

Driver Two was shaking his head. 'Sorry, Chewy, there will be no 'Whoo Hoo' when you are with me, mate. It could get dangerous. We don't know what we are dealing with or who. I've met Lofty and Lardy, so I must stay in the car. You and Sandy will be in the firing line so to speak. I don't want to have that con-versation with Nic when it all goes pear-shaped.

'Touché, Driver Two.'

The five of them returned to the apartment, where Rose donned her 'Three French Bens' uniform and helped Sandy into the old woman's suit. 'You scared, Rose?'

'Of what? Having to speak French to a room full of drunk and bloated Casino goers, or that we are staying in an apartment with Nic?'

'Rose, now you are scaring me, but at least we don't have Benoit Trudeau with us in here, though that would make exciting gossip for the ladies at our hairdressing salon, wouldn't it?'

'Yes. So, are you good to go, Mrs Buxom?'

'I think so. What about you?'

'Oui.'

Rose and Sandy came back out of the room, and Nic smiled. Driver Two stifled a laugh. 'What's so funny, Driver Two?'

'You look like my mother.'

Nic lowered the mood. 'OK, guys, I don't want you to do this if you feel unsafe. It's not the movies. If you do something wrong, you could get hurt. There's no pause and re-set button.'

Driver Two nodded. 'Roger that. You told me there is no 'me' only 'we'. I'll take it that means 'we' must always feel safe. If I get a hint of anything else, we get out.' Nic nodded. 'Let's get this underway. Can you drop us off at the Casino? Then, you guys can go back to look for the lost dog. Remember, avoid Mrs Brosnan. Start at the other end of the street.'

Driver Two dropped Rose and Nic at the New Crowd Casino, and they went directly to the restaurant. Ben Patterson was waiting for them.

'Bonjour Mademoiselle Rose and Monsieur Nicolas. I'm not sure if Benoit will be attending tonight's session. François Benson has told me he'll be late as he isn't feeling well, so I am still deciding if we will open. I've already run it past the Casino people, and I could blame it on the damn Bank not having the EFTPOS terminal installed.'

Nic nodded, and Rose looked at Ben. *'Excusez moi Monsieur Patterson, est-ce que vous parlez?'*

Ben looked over at Rose. 'I think you just asked me if I speak French. The answer is no, Rose. I don't have to, as that is part of the 'Three French Bens' charm. I would guess it's most likely why Benoit has gone missing. He probably thought we all spoke French, and when he found out I didn't, he's gone off in a huff.'

Nic looked at him. 'I don't think so, Ben, and there's more to it than that. He's a good friend of mine, and something fishy is going on with your restaurant that he just invested two hundred and fifty thousand dollars into.'

Ben looked over to Nic, suddenly realising the seriousness of the situation made a twirl motion with his finger, and then Lofty appeared from within the restaurant. 'This is my brother, and he does the fish supplies. If you have a problem with that, ask him. So, maybe if you don't get out of my face, Nicolas, your pretty French maid might cop my fist in her little nose.'

Rose whispered to Nic. 'This isn't good, Nic,' and she stepped backwards.

Nic looked over at the two men. 'It is good, Rose, as it means only one of them is guarding Benoit.' Nic stepped forward, holding his finger up and his phone to his ear. 'Good to go.'

Ben P looked at him. 'What's that about Nicolas?'

'Well, two things. One: My friends have just told the Police to enter the house at No. 3, where you have been holding Benoit Trudeau for the last week or so, and Two: The Casino has just been informed about the fish supply scam you and your brother have been running here for the last couple of years.'

'I don't think so, Nicolas, and you might want to re-think what you are saying, especially with your pretty little lady standing next to you, whilst my brother is standing next to me.'

Rose looked at him and whispered. 'Sorry, Ben, I think it's all over, baby blue.' Her comment took Nic aback. 'Wow, that's a line from a song Rose.'

Ben P looked at them. 'Why are you two jabbering about music trivia to me? I don't care about that crap. I want you out of my face and out of my restaurant. Take care of this, will you, bro?' Lofty moved forward and took a fighting stance. 'OK, Mister Whoever you are, I'll give you a fist full of fury if you don't move out of the way. Let me introduce you to....'

Nic smiled. 'Hey, that's another good film, Lofty, I believe it was one of Bruce Lee's back in seventy-two, one of his very early ones, but before you go all 'Kato attack' on me, can I introduce *you* to my right thumb? This little guy here is a registered weapon with the Tom Thumb Teetotallers. If you're nice to it, he may let you breathe normally a little longer; if not, you might need to lie down.'

The tall man lunged, and Nic weaved out of the way, then he jabbed his thumb into the man's lower back area. Lofty rubbed the spot and squared up again, but this time, Nic thrust his thumb forward sharply into the man's throat and swept his legs out from under him. The tall man went down gasping for air, and Nic softly held the back of his neck, guiding him to the ground. 'Breathe, mate. It will hurt for a while, but eventually, you'll be able to suck on a straw and swallow a bit easier.'

Rose looked at him. 'You said that you don't do violence, Nic. What was that?'

'Sorry, Rose. I think I said I don't do guns. Anyhow, I did warn him about my right thumb, and Ben did threaten to re-arrange your pretty retrousse nose. I like your nose just the way it is.' Rose looked down at Lofty gasping for air. 'Was it jujitsu or something?'

Nic then attempted the classic James Bond statement in his best Scottish lilt: 'Shaken, and stirred.' Ben also looked down at his brother on the floor, then up at Rose. 'I'm warning you, young lady, take control of your guy; otherwise, you are sacked.'

Nic shook his head. 'Sorry, Ben 'the Fish Food Fraudster', this time it's over. I hope you haven't spent Benoit's share yet. I think he may want his money back.'

This time, Ben P smiled. 'I don't think so, Nic. I have a watertight Partnership Agreement with François

Benson and your mate, so they are stuck with me unless they get a majority.'

Rose looked at him. 'Do your sums, you dope. If you get two of them against you, they have the majority by one. There are only Three French Bens, not a bunch of Bens making the decisions.'

François Benson then walked up behind the group. 'Bonjour, Mademoiselle Rose and Monsieur Nicolas. You wanted to talk to me about rescinding the Partnership Agreement?'

Ben P smiled again. 'Your play Nicolas No-Clue.'

François Benson, being the only real Frenchman there, continued: 'I've just had a lovely chat with my Lawyer. Did you know, Benoit and I used the same Legal firm, and in hindsight, it didn't make sense, but at least we didn't use the same lawyer. Ben P is right, and it is a good Agreement, but...'

Ben P waited, smiled and waited for François to continue.

'Yes, certainly it is two against one, so Ben, you are out. Benoit and I had a lovely chat about the fish supply and substitution racket you and your brother have been running. This was my restaurant, too, and I am French, and we can get nasty. You are an insult to our culture.'

Rose took a deep breath, and Nic muttered. *'C'est bientot fini, Rose.'*

François nodded. 'Hey, that's a nice French dialect, Nic, and yes, it's almost over. Besides, I already have another partner to replace you.' The Frenchman took a moment. 'Ben Patterson, you Frenchman wanna be: '*Va te faire cuire un oeuf.*'

Rose whispered to Nic. 'Oh, that was nasty. François just told Ben to 'go and cook himself an egg'. We use slightly different words when we tell someone to shove off. The French are so polite.'

Five Casino Security Officers were now standing beside François, and he nodded to Ben and down at Lofty. 'Please remove these two from your premises. They have overstayed their welcome at the New Crowd Casino.'

The Officers began to manhandle Ben and helped Lofty to his feet. Ben looked at François, 'This isn't the end, you stupid little Frenchman. I still have the money.'

Francois smiled at his comment, then continued; 'Sorry, Ben, and about that, when we opened the new business account, I transferred Benoit's share back to the lawyers' Trust Account. It's being held in trust pending the mandatory three months' business performance. That part wasn't written in the Partnership Agreement, but when Benoit informed me of his suspicions, I thought it would be a good idea.'

Ben sneered at him, and François added: 'Oh, here's a business tip for the naïve. Don't authorise any one person to transfer funds around. Oh, and here's another: pay more attention to the Bank Account balances and less to ripping people off with fishy business practices.'

Nic nodded in agreement. 'Touché, Monsieur Benson. Where to from here then, François?'

'Benoit and I have agreed to delay the opening for another two weeks whilst we get this fishy mess sorted out and get another fish supplier. Chrissie Benaud is the new incoming partner. We are also changing the name to 'Trois Bens Francaise.''

Rose looked at him. 'That means the same thing as 'Three French Bens,' François.'

'Oui Mademoiselle, but it sounds so much more French, doesn't it?'

CHAPTER 8

Nic had called Driver Two to come and collect them, and return to the apartment. 'How's Benoit, mate? Was it his blood on the carpet?'

'Nope, he's all good. It turns out it was Lardy's, after all. He copped a wooden drawer in the nose when they were chucking around all the furniture, looking for the thumb drive. Benoit interrupted them, and that's how they grabbed him so easily.'

'So, they knew about the thumb drive then?'

'Yep, but it wasn't Benoit's; it was Monsieur Benson's. The two Frenchmen hit it off when they met, as well as being real Frenchmen, they are both massive 'Star Wars fans. They were using the thumb drive to collect and store information about the restaurant. François couldn't tell Ben P what he was looking into, so Benoit had it for safekeeping. Ben Patterson was always going to be in trouble.'

'Otherwise, he's OK then?'

'Yes, apparently, his captors were very partial to French Food. Benoit convinced them he wouldn't try to escape, so he fed them, and they looked after him well. It was more about Ben Patterson trying to work out what to do with the fish supply issue, rather than holding Benoit to ransom or anything more sinister.'

Rose looked at Nic. 'So, we'll still have to live together in the apartment even though our roles at the restaurant are already over? Does that mean I finally get to meet the really, really good-looking alleged cousin of Justin Trudeau?'

'Yep, but you might have to line up to assist with Benoit's recuperation, though, Sandy has been with him all afternoon after they rescued him.'

'Damn you, Nic.'

Driver Two pulled the car into the Tyrian turnout. Rose and Nic stepped out, and he drove away. 'He was a good find, wasn't he, Nic? I'd say he's probably a better driver than his brother in Adelaide, and at least Driver Two, living in Melbourne, knew to look out for trams.'

'That's funny, Rose. I like both of them, and it's great that we all get along. It's always hard to get the right people to work with, and once you get the people, will they play nicely with all the rest of the people? Sometimes you don't know people.'

'How do you come up with all these words of wisdom? You must be exhausted.'

'Speaking of being exhausted. I hope Sandy didn't lie on the couch you bought for the apartment. She tends to go to sleep on them very quickly.'

'Yes, to that too. I assume the couch can return to your St Kilda house when we finish in the apartment?'

'Yep. I paid for it after all, didn't I?'

'Yes, Nic, but think of all the points you get with all the Credit Card spending that Sandy and I do. Win, win, I'd say.'

'Funny again, Rose, and a word of warning, if I may, when you meet Benoit, please don't stare. He knows he's good-looking and that he's French. He doesn't need to be reminded about it.'

They took the elevator and soon arrived at the apartment. Sandy opened the door and let them in. 'How is the patient?'

Sandy nodded. 'He is having a shower at the moment.' Rose and Sandy simultaneously raised their hands to their mouths with the same reaction. Nic then ventured towards his suite and called back: 'Hey, what am I, chopped liver? Do you swoon like that when I have a shower?'

Rose called back. 'No, Benoit, on the other hand.....'

Benoit eventually emerged from the bedroom, fully dressed in French couture, even down to the little black chapeau. Nic was behind him, also well dressed, but Benoit looked like a catwalk model.

Benoit nodded at Rose. *Enchante Mademoiselle Rose. Je suis ravi de vous e rencontrer.'*

'Pleased to meet you finally, too, Benoit. Nic has told us so little about you.'

'Rose.'

'Yes, Nic?'

'Behave.'

Sandy looked at Rose and used her old woman voice. 'What'd he say, luv? It sounded French, so I didn't quite catch it.'

'He said, 'He's pleased to meet me, Sandy.' And hey, that's not fair; you have been with him all afternoon whilst I slaved away working at the restaurant.'

Benoit looked at Rose. 'It's not open yet, Mademoiselle Rose.'

Rose was about to respond when the doorbell rang. They looked at each other, and Benoit smiled. 'I'll get it. Likely for me.' He opened the door, and a woman with two small children stood there. The children looked about six years old. 'Hi Papa, we've all missed you waiting at the other house, so Mummy brought us around here.'

Benoit scooped up the boy and girl and hugged them tightly. The woman moved around him, went up to Nic, and they did the European double air kiss, then she looked towards Sandy and Rose.

'Hello, I am Gabrielle, Benoit's wife, and these are our children, Jean-Louis and Madelaine. We've just arrived from Canberra. We had to wait for the school term to finish before moving to Melbourne. Nic has told me so much about both of you two. Thank you for looking after Benoit, too, Sandy. It must have been awful to see him like that.'

Sandy nodded. 'My pleasure, Gabrielle; however, Nic didn't mention Benoit was married with children.'

'Oh, it's all over Facebook. We've kept in touch over the last couple of months. Long distance relationships are a real drag.'

Sandy looked at Nic. 'Facebook? You said the French don't do Facebook.'

'Oh, sorry, I did say that, but I didn't want you drooling all over my phone.'

Benoit looked at his family, then at Nic. 'So, are we good to go then? Are you OK if I take my family back to St Kilda's house?'

Nic nodded. 'Yep, we can work out the lease later, but there's no hurry. Get your family settled. Oh, but I have a favour to ask, given that the restaurant isn't opening for another couple of weeks. Are you free Wednesday to join us at the Mercedes-Benz Fashion Show?'

'Sure. What'll I need to do, Monsieur Nic?'

'I'd like you to stand next to a Mercedes car for a few hours and take over when Rose and Sandy need a break. It might be good if Gabrielle can make it, too. I can introduce her to some people in Melbourne. Just be back here around nine a.m. on Wednesday.'

'Oui Nic, and merci beaucoup, for everything.'

Benoit then led his family out of the apartment and Sandy looked at Nic. 'What was that all about? I thought you didn't like to be around really good-looking people, and now you have Benoit to be a fashion model with us.'

'Yep, remember it's my show, and my friend Douglas was interested in upgrading to a Rolls Royce Phantom.'

Rose looked at him. 'I don't think that deserves a response, Nic.'

'Thanks, but I knew you would understand. I didn't ask how the Mrs Buxom disguise went, Sandy. You guys distracted me by going all 'goo-goo eyes' at Benoit.'

'That's not fair. We stopped as soon as we found out he was married.'

Nic looked at Sandy. 'As if. So how did it go?'

'It went well, and it's surprising how much people tell you when you're dressed as someone they aren't threatened by. Even when we got to the house where we found Benoit, he answered the door. Lardy came outside with him to look for the lost dog. That's when Driver Two made his move.'

'Did it get ugly?'

'Nope. Lardy realised who we were and who we were there for, and he realised the gig was up. It was all done quietly and easily. Chewy was disappointed, though, as he wanted to use his lightsaber on him. I told him that threatening to hit someone with a plastic tube wasn't a good idea. Especially if they have a gun.'

'Did he have a gun?'

'Nope, but Driver Two did threaten to punch Lardy in the nose if he didn't give up Benoit. He seemed to take that well, given a bandage was still on his nose.'

Nic smiled. 'Good job, guys. We can wrap this one up, and if anyone wants to eat, let's not have fish and chips. It's not just the restaurants that mess with the fish supply chain.'

It was Wednesday morning, and Gabrielle and Benoit arrived at the apartment as directed. He was dressed in French Riviera Fashion couture, and Rose and Sandy wore the Bass & Side outfits. Nic gave them all the once over. 'Boy, I feel like Orphan Annie standing next to you guys. I now understand why you didn't invite me to your thirtieth, Sandy. I can't compete against the beautiful people.'

'Boo Hoo, Nic. Besides it's Rose's thirtieth soon, if you're nice to us you just might get an invite.'

Rose smiled. 'As if.'

The group made their way downstairs to the foyer. Driver Two was waiting for them in a stretched pink Hummer. 'I'd been talking to my brother, and he told me you bought a Hummer for this Douglas guy after you sold him the Mercedes 300SL. So, when I saw this one available to drive, I couldn't resist it. I hope you don't mind?' Nic nodded. 'There's a little more to the story Driver Two, but maybe for another day.'

They arrived at the Melbourne Entertainment Centre, alighted from the massive vehicle, and Nic's friend

Douglas was there to greet them. He re-introduced his friend Elliott, and the two elderly gentlemen put their heads into the Hummer and went to step inside. 'Can we look inside this beast, Nic as the one you bought for us is only half this size.'

Nic nodded, and the two gentlemen stepped in; then Rose heard both men shriek.

'I would say they saw Benoit.' Sandy nodded in confirmation. 'Yep, I would say so.' They overheard a comment from Douglas. 'Oh, my, my. Who are you? Nic didn't tell me about the little surprise inside for us.' They heard Benoit's response. 'Bonjour. I am Benoit Trudeau, and this is Gabrielle, my wife.' Rose looked at Nic; he was shaking his head. 'Don't worry, Nic, at least you have us two.'

The Fashion Show was a success, and the talk of the show was the Mercedes 300SL and the new French couple in town, Benoit and Gabrielle Trudeau. 'Trois Bens Francaise' was informally launched on the final day. Rose was saying goodbye when she remembered about the Rolls Royce. 'So Nic, did you have any success with Douglas and the car upgrade?'

'Nope. Douglas seemed to be distracted for some reason. Maybe if the Rolls Royce Phantom spoke French and not Upper-Class Brit, I might've had a chance.'

CHAPTER 9

Rose, Sandy and Nic were now back at the Tyrian apartment winding things down when a phone rang. It played the theme of the 'Lone Ranger.' Nic did a little jig as the phone rang. 'That's a great ringtone, Sandy.'

'It's the ringtone for everything. I can't remember how to change it.' Sandy answered the phone and listened intently, and then a look of horror crossed her face. Sandy hung up in tears.

Rose leaned toward her. 'What's happened, Sandy? Who was it?'

She took a deep breath. 'It's Dave from next door; he's in hospital. He was run over trying to stop a Repossession Agent from taking our new car from outside our house. That was his mum on the phone. He was more worried about leaving our cat to fend for himself rather than getting into the ambulance. She's gone over there to feed Dog.'

Nic responded first. 'That's interesting since the car isn't even in your name. It's registered with Nic Thorn & Associates. It sounds like the woman with your stolen ID has popped her head up again. I reckon

I know how she did it. She would've taken the VIN details when she was at your party and used the car as collateral for a loan. Excuse me whilst I make a call.' Nic moved off to his bedroom suite, and Sandy continued: 'Rose, they must have broken into the garage to take the car. I usually lock the roller door, but maybe this time, I didn't. I can't remember if I locked the house either. We need to go to Brisbane, Rose.'

Rose nodded. 'Sure. Benoit, Gabrielle and Chewy could wind this up anyway. Remember our agreement with Nic? We do it if you or I ever need to go back home. It's part of the reason we have his Credit Cards.'

Nic returned the call. 'My guys did a Property Register Search. The Sunshire Credit Union has lodged a charge on the vehicle when a loan was taken out against it. I guess someone used your stolen ID to transfer the ownership over to your name. They then paid the stamp duty and used it as collateral. Now that the loan is in default, they have repossessed the car.'

'How does this stuff happen, Nic?'

'Not often, but it's due to a lack of security protocols. The Credit Unions are clambering over each other to write the business scraps that the Big Four Banks don't do. If a borrower can put pressure on to get it done quickly or provide all the paperwork that looks so good the lender doesn't even bother to do a visual inspection so the deal gets done. Most of these lenders process their online applications and some dude sitting somewhere ticks all the boxes, then 'ta-dah' the money pops up in the account to buy the car.'

Rose nodded. 'How do we track it down? And how quickly can we get back to Brisbane to sort it out?'

'I'm packed if you are…. I'll ring Driver Two. I can have us on tonight's six-thirty flight to Brisbane. Is that quick enough?'

Sandy took a breath. 'Thanks, Nic.' Nic continued, 'If it was a her, this woman is very good and game. She would know that her guy at the Community Bank in Brisbane is out of action, so she's stepped up and used an alternative funding source. I'll get Chewy to see if he can find out how the money was borrowed, and by the time we land in Brisbane, he should have some leads for us, despite an ongoing desire to be a Jedi Knight.'

Sandy nodded. 'That's from 'Star Wars', Rose.'

'Thanks, I figured as much, Sandy.'

They finished packing, and Driver Two collected them in the same stretched Hummer again. 'Sorry, Nic. I haven't taken it back as yet. I just dropped Elliott and Douglas at the Grand Hyatt, and we took a little detour around Melbourne. He'll get back to you about buying that Rolls Royce Phantom. We just had to drive along Swann Rd, Richmond too, had a bit of damn car trouble outside No. 420 though.'

Nic nodded. 'All forgiven, mate, and thanks, as I'm aware the location of the Rolls Royce Dealer here in Melbourne is at 420 Swann Road.'

They arrived at the airport, and Driver Two pulled the Hummer to a stop in the departure drop-off just as paparazzi leapt at them from the sidewalk. A photographer was at the open door with his camera flashing. Nic stepped out first, then Rose and Sandy. They shielded their eyes from the ongoing flashes. 'C'mon mate, we are no-one. Just going about our business.'

The photographer snapped away. 'You might be a no-one, but those two are from the Mercedes-Benz Fashion Show. They spent their days looking after the 300SL. They are super-models who looked after a supercar.'

Driver Two stepped out of the car and stood to his full two-metre height. 'Mate, they may be super-models, but I'm Superman.' He stepped towards the photographer, but Nic held him back. 'That's OK. It's a bit of fun. Just find out whom he works for in case they want to know who they are being chased by.' Driver Two nodded, let the photographer do his thing, bade them farewell, climbed into the Hummer and drove off.

The trio went directly to the QANTAS Lounge and waited for their flight, and when they boarded, they were again sitting in the same row. Nic was in the middle, and Rose and Sandy were on either side. Half an hour into the flight, they were asleep against his shoulders. His arms were pinned to his side, so he couldn't attract the steward's attention. 'Damn you two, I need a Chai Tea.'

A Flight Attendant eventually walked past and chortled. 'Hello, Mister Thorn. Nice to see you again. I have a long straw if you would like a Chai Tea.'

Nic woke the two Sleeping Beauties just before the arrival was announced. They took a taxi back to West End, and Nic offered to stay the night, so the women made up the couch for him. They all decided to have an early night, and the women went to bed.

A few minutes later, Dog sat on Nic's chest as he lay on the couch. 'Hey guys, I can't move. There is a big purring, furry lump sitting on me. I can't breathe.... I know you can hear me...guys....help...'

CHAPTER 10

In the morning, Nic heard back from the Repossession Agent, and whilst they were sympathetic, they even quoted the old chestnut of 'due processes' back to him. He was not even permitted to view the car or know its location.

Sandy didn't take it well. 'This is stupid. Surely, you can't just accept what they're saying. I don't believe you don't know where it is. Can we go and steal it back from them.'

'I can't do that. It's not my scene. I may bend the law sometimes, but I don't break it. I know where it is, and the Repo Agent will take care of it for me for a week or two while this is sorted out. Chewy will let me know if anything else happens.'

Sandy took a deep breath. 'Can you at least put us out of our misery then? Where is the car, and how do you know it won't be sold? What's to stop them from selling the car and giving the lenders back the difference?'

'Well, the car is at Brendale, but they must obey the law too. There is a twenty-one-day claim process to follow. Still, in this case, as fraud has been involved in transferring the car's title, it won't be a good look for the Repo Agent or the Sunshire Credit Union to do anything with it. Besides, we have another job to look into if you are interested?'

Sandy nodded. 'OK, fine then. So, what's this new thing? Are we likely to get all wet and muddy again?'

'Well, where we are going, they generally see a lot of rain and big bulls. The town has about seven bull statues scattered around it.'

Rose held out her hand and counted down on her fingers. 'So, it's not Hawaii, Maldives, or Fiji. Is it even overseas this time?'

'Nope, sorry, but we are chasing down a couple of duffers, who like to go duffing.'

'Hang onto that thought, Rose. Let me google it.' Sandy searched for the word in her phone. 'OK, duffing is beating people up in the UK, drinking beer in Homer Simpson land, and it's cattle stealing. 'Duffing' is cattle rustling in Australia, and that's no bull.'

'Yep, so strap on your spurs and ride high in the saddle, guys, because Nic Thorn and his associates are going to Rockhampton, and that's the good news.'

Sandy smiled. 'Whoa, Nic, what else do you have in store for us then? Do I need to bring my stock whip?'

'We'll catch up with Sticks Out and our singing mate, Carly. They're working with me in a trio tribute band. We're called 'The Dusty Spring Fields' and will perform at the one and only Rockhampton Rodeo Show.'

'How is that good news?'

'We need a couple of roadies, and you two will fit the bill. You might even have to get on stage with us and belt out a few tunes. Have you ever heard of Slim Dusty or Dusty Springfield?' Rose nodded. 'Slim Dusty, I have. He did one called 'The Pub with no Beer', a real tearjerker, and Dusty Springfield did the song 'Wishin' and Hopin'. They used it at the start of the Julia Roberts film, 'My Best Friend's Wedding."

Nic nodded. 'You're right, Rose. You've certainly broadened your musical horizon since you met me.'

Sandy piped up. 'Actually, no. Nic, that wedding movie with Julia Roberts and Cameron Diaz, was on TV a couple of weeks ago. They used 'A Pub with no Beer' at the Castlemaine Brewery at Milton when the delivery drivers went on strike last month.'

Rose looked at them, 'OK. Maybe one day I'll re-member why I need to know more about music and movies, and stuff.'

'Sure, let me know when that day is, and I'll get a bottle of Dom Perignon to celebrate.' Rose grinned. 'Thanks, Nic. You know me, I have a champagne taste on your beer budget.' Sandy interrupted the banter. 'So, what's this thing in Rockhampton all about? Surely, we're not going all that way to watch you wail up on a stage and chase around a herd of cattle?'

'It's a bit more than that, Sandy, but the Band is

my cover-up there and will be fun. The cattle thing is serious, and the Queensland Department of Agriculture and Fisheries has asked us to follow up on some leads. Stock theft is escalating, becoming a big issue when times are good, things get busy and beef prices are up. They can't be everywhere, so they've called us to investigate. And *that's* no bull.'

Rose shook her head. 'It certainly sounds like it. How do they steal them? Get a big truck and whisper to the herd that they can offer them a better life in the field of cow dreams?'

'Nope, they've *moooved* on by then. It's mostly done on horseback as they walk the herd to the pickup spot. Then grab the fifty or so cattle, remove the ear tags, or re-brand them. The cattle feed lots up there are so huge that once you get someone on the inside, you can access the un-branded cattle without question. They feed them for fifty or sixty days, then on-sell them for just under a thousand dollars.'

Rose shook her head. 'So, when they go to market, no one bothers to find out if the feedlot owned them in the first place? That's dumb. What's the fine anyway?'

'Can be up to a thousand dollars per animal, but the main issue is that the barbeque has gone cold by the time the theft is reported.'

Rose smiled. 'Yes, and who likes cold beef anyway.'

Nic shrugged. 'If you guys are in, what will happen

to Dog? Can Dave from next door look after him again?'

'We can get Sandy's friend 'Pucker' to stay here. She gets on well with Dave. It's so funny to watch her reaction to him, too. You know she likes to kiss everyone she meets on the mouth? He gets in first, and she tries to run away.'

'Good to know, guys.'

'OK, it sounds like a plan. Sticks Out, Carly, Crusoe and I will go up in a campervan for the gig. I'll get another one organised for you two.'

'Who's Crusoe?'

'Sorry, it's William Robinson. He's our new sound guy. Don't call him 'Danger'. It annoys him. That's why everyone calls him 'Crusoe.''

Sandy stood up and waved her arms before her, mimicking the robot for the 60's TV show. 'That's almost as funny as 'Pucker' Nic. 'Danger Will Robinson, 'Danger'. Parents can be cruel with children's names, can't they?'

Rose looked at them. 'Yes, they can, but what's it to do with a robot?'

Nic stared at her, then stood up. 'And with that comment, I think I'll be going. I have to practice with Sticks Out and Carly for the gig. Oh, and thanks for arranging the styling at my house in Brookwater. It's now under contract.' Nic started singing the Abba song: "Money, money, money" and then added: 'especially when I am the rich man.'

Sandy sat down and shook her head. 'That was supposed to be a line from an ABBA song, Rose.'

'I thought it was, but what a terrible rendition. I hope the Dusty Spring Fields don't use it, as I don't want to hear him sing it again.' Nic began to move away. 'Wow, that's nasty, and I won't give you a bonus for staging my house.'

'That's OK, but we can't remember you ever paying us yet for anything or ever giving us a bonus.'

Sandy's phone started ringing, so she headed inside, and Rose watched Nic getting into an Uber when Dog suddenly bounded up the stairs. The cat had a big stick in his mouth, and he moved to the decking rail and looked over to see a Labrador down below looking forlorn. Sandy returned. 'I told them I had company and they hung up; they may've been trying to sell me a dead parrot.'

A few days later, an email arrived from Nic that contained the lyrics of two Dusty Springfield songs: 'I Only Want to Be with You' and 'Wishin and Hopin' with a browser link to the artist singing the songs.

'Please Listen and learn these, guys. It's going to be a hoot.'

Rose and Sandy were horrified and immediately sent a text back.

'But we don't sing.'

A week later, around 7 p.m., Sandy and Rose caught the ferry to the Jazz Club at Kangaroo Point to listen to 'The Dusty Spring Fields'. They met up with Carly,

Sticks Out, Nic and Crusoe. There was a small crowd there as well. Carly readied herself on the keyboard and moved up to the microphone.

'Hi, and thanks for coming tonight. We've been working on a small Dusty Springfield medley for the Rockhampton Show and six Slim Dusty songs. This will be a rehearsal for our show. Oh, and the two ladies that have just come in are our backup singers. This will be their first performance, so please go easy on them.' The trio started with 'Son of a Preacher Man', then onto 'The Look of Love'. 'You Don't Have to Say You Love Me' was next. Carly stopped, took a breath, and there was applause from the audience: 'OK. These next two songs are just as well-known as those heart-breakers. Let us introduce you to Cilla Black and Cilla Presley. They aren't their real names, folks.'

Rose looked at Sandy. 'I think she means us. Are you ready?'

'Nope, but let's do it anyway. I am tired of listening to those two songs, so let's see what we can do with them with a real Band and microphones instead of the hairbrushes and full-length mirrors.'

Nic stepped out and helped them to the stage. 'This will be fun.'

Rose and Sandy laughed nervously, and Sticks Out started the backbeat on the drums. Carly pointed them towards a third microphone set up on stage. Sandy tapped the unit to see if it was turned on. Crusoe gave them the thumbs up. 'Guys, can you speak into the microphone one at a time? I have to recheck the levels. Just say 'check one, two, three.'' Rose went first, then Sandy.

'OK, good. Let's go to the first song. Start the beat, Sticks.'

The band started playing, and Carly began singing the song however Rose and Sandy stood there, so Carly gave Crusoe the 'cut' signal and looked to the audience. 'Sorry guys. Hey Cilla's, you're on from the first verse and clap immediately at the end of each line. Lots of Aahs and Oohs, too, please. It's a bouncy tune, so enjoy.' Carly nodded to Sticks Out to start again. Rose and Sandy took a deep breath and stood on each side of the microphone. The song began again, and the look on Nic's face was one of amazement when they sang.

When the song was at the slower third verse, Carly stood back from the microphone and let Rose and Sandy take it on themselves, and then Carly joined in for the last verse. They sang the first verse again and wound it down. The small audience gave them a standing ovation.

'Nic, when did they learn to sing? I've known Sandy for years. I never knew.'

'Neither did I, Carly.'

'Right, Cilla's, onto the next one. *Wishin and Hopin.*''

This song was even better than the last. Sandy and Rose used the theatrics from the Julia Roberts film and had the audience join in, too. When the song ended, they curtseyed and moved off the stage. Carly nodded to them. 'Wow. I mean it, thanks, and when I need backup singers. I know where to go first.'

Rose and Sandy sat back on their stools, and a man came up. 'Hi, ladies. I really liked that. Carly said it was your first time, too. Congrats. I run this place and am always looking for acts. Do you perform professionally anywhere at the moment?'

'No, we don't. When Carly said it was our first time, she meant it. That was the first time we've ever sung live or with a band.'

'So, do you have a manager or anything?'

'Sort of; the rhythm guitarist is our manager.'

'OK, I'll talk to him about getting you a gig here if you want. Do you guys have a band name or any-thing?'

'Err, well no, but I'm Rose E, and this is Sandra D.'

Nic had meantime moved off the stage as Carly was having a drink. He'd overheard what was going on and moved towards them. 'Sorry mate, not yet, as they don't have a song list. It's still a work in progress. The Band has the Rockhampton Rodeo Show next week, so let's get together and we can talk after that.' The man looked toward Nic. 'OK. So, Rose. Is she like your partner then?'

Nic smiled. 'Not likely, just another one of my many groupies.'

Rose whispered. 'Damn, you Nic.'

Nic smiled, turned away and joined Carly back on stage. They finished the remainder of the Dusty Springfield songs, and Sticks Out stood up from behind the drums. 'My turn now. This will be slightly different as Nic, Carly, and I will do harmonies. We've put together new arrangements for the Slim Dusty songs. We know the great man's songs deserve to remain untouched, so please bear with us as we think our sound compliments his style.'

They started a three-part harmony of 'Along the Road to Gundagai' and followed up with a medley including 'Pub with No Beer'. When they got around to the last song, 'Waltzing Matilda,' Carly asked Rose and Sandy to join them on stage and when the song finished, the crowd were again on their feet.

The show finished at 9 p.m., and Rose and Sandy did their thing as first-time roadies, packing everything up and helping everyone down and out. Sticks came up to them. 'That was great, guys, and thanks for coming to the gig too. It will make it a great weekend, and whatever you guys have done for Nic, it's made a big difference. He's changed and seems to be enjoying life much more.'

Sandy nodded. 'Yes, I guess it's been around ten months since we met him. Did you know he uses the Vita Brevis dating app? That's where he found Rose.'

'Nope, I didn't think that was his scene.' Sticks looked over to Nic. 'Since when did you start using a dating app to get your kicks?'

'I only used it once but stopped looking after I met Rose, and then I met Sandy. Those two are all that I need in my life at the moment. Are you two good to go?'

Rose and Sandy nodded. 'It's OK, Nic, we'll catch the ferry home.'

'Nope, you are our backup singers and must avoid letting the cold air get to your throats. Besides, when did you learn to sing?' The Uber arrived, they climbed in together, and Rose continued. 'Well, you gave us a week to learn the songs, so we both got lessons. It's all about the image and performance, you know, 'every night is an opening night', that sort of thing.'

Nic smiled. 'You're right, as there ain't no time to 'fake it until you make it' in my line of work, is there? Oh, by the way, can either of you drive a cattle truck or ride a horse?'

CHAPTER 11

It was early morning. Rose and Sandy were waiting for the others to arrive as arrangements had been made to meet outside their West End home, and then they'd decide how to share the seven-hour drive to Rockhampton. A Land Cruiser Troopy was the first to appear. It was packed to the hilt with music equipment, and a folded-up canvas tent was on the roof. Nic jumped out of the passenger side. 'This one sleeps five, but we think the three men will share.'

The vehicle to turn up next was an early model Volkswagen Kombi. Carly was driving, and Sticks Out was on the passenger side. Nic nodded over to it. 'This is Carly's dad's old Kombi. They had it decked out with all the mod-cons. Two single beds over the wheels and the front and back bench seats make a double bed. You three will sleep in that one.'

'So, where's the six-star Winnebago then? Still to arrive?'

'Sorry, Sandy. We might have to rough it this time.'

Carly, Sticks Out, and Crusoe helped load their

luggage into the Kombi, and Rose went up to Nic. 'Are they all in on the cattle rustling thing too?'

'Nope. Carly isn't yet, but I might have to bring her in any way. She's the only one that can ride a horse.'

'What about Sticks Out and Crusoe?'

'Sticks has an idea what I get up to with these investigations, but we might have to keep Crusoe out of the loop. That way, one person can deny everything if we get caught. This one could get ugly too as sometimes real cowboys turn out to be real cowboys and don't like being outsmarted by us city folk.'

'Who's going to drive the Cattle Truck then?'

'It's all organised. I've had a guy working in the All Cattle Transporters business for a few months. According to the Department of Agriculture, that's the business linked to cattle rustling.'

Sandy nodded. 'Hey, I've forgotten something,' then dashed back inside, and a couple of minutes later, she returned, yielding a stock whip. 'I use it as a leash for Dog and thought it might be good to bring to Rockhampton with us.' Sandy ushered everyone out of the way, and a couple of seconds later the whip cracked in the early morning mist.

Nic was impressed with her whipping. 'C'mon, Wo-Man from Snowy River, you can put it down now. We have to get going.'

Meanwhile, Dave had ambled over from next door to see what was happening. He was walking with a cane and had one arm in a sling. 'Go on, off you guys go. Have fun without me.'

Nic looked at him. 'Thanks for what you did, Dave. I hope 'Pucker' is going to look after you.' And with that, Sandy's hockey friend came to the front door. She was sniffling and didn't look like her usual cheerful self. 'Hi, Nig. I've gud a bad gold. Won't be uble to give all you guys a kiz for good-lugg.'

Nic smiled. 'Maybe next time, Pucker.'

The three women climbed into the Kombi. Sandy was in the passenger seat and Rose in the back whilst the men went to the Land Cruiser. Crusoe beeped the horn, and they watched the Kombi head off. Nic looked back to Pucker and Dave and saw that he'd moved closer to her, and she tried to escape him. 'I haven't given you a good morning kiss yet, Pucker. Come on, pucker up.'

About an hour into the journey, Rose's phone chirped, and Nic called: 'We're detouring into Gympie to catch up with some other musicians. It's about an hour away. We might change drivers and the seating arrangements around, and by the way, stop singing those ABBA songs so loudly. We can hear you from back here.'

'Funny, Nic. I thought it was you snoring, but then realised it's the little Volksy engine making all the noise.'

Rose looked at Carly. 'Did you get that, Carly? We're stopping in Gympie.'

Carly nodded. 'So, what's this thing with you guys and Nic? Sandy has tried to explain that you both work for him, but I don't quite get it. I mean, the guy is hot and everything, too.'

'Err, well, we do work for him.'

Sandy turned to Rose and nodded. 'Nic told me we can fill her in, Rose.'

'OK then, Carly. Nic is like a Private Investigator. He gets called in to investigate scams, frauds and stuff like that. He also buys stuff, sells stuff, and does other stuff too. In this case, the Department of Agriculture has asked him to look into some cattle rustling that's going on near Rockhampton. He's using the band thing as a cover.'

Carly nodded. 'OK. So, as well as looking hot, he does that stuff, too? Luckily, he doesn't have a bushy moustache and isn't wearing Tommy Bahama. He could be a real Magnum P.I., you know, like the handsome Tom Sellick from the '80s.'

Rose added. 'Yes, he had a great car too. An '84 Ferrari 308, and the TV show was filmed in Hawaii. What a show, what a car, what a guy and what an island. Nic keeps promising to take us there.'

Carly continued: 'Tom can park his driving shoes under my bed any day.' Rose piped up from the back seat. 'Eeww Carly, he's like over eighty now.'

They pulled into the Gympie Showgrounds and

met up with other bands going to the Rockhampton Show. Sticks Out jumped down from the Troopy and called out, 'It's going to be a convoy,' then pulled a pair of drumsticks from his back pocket and started a beat on a rubbish bin. Someone grabbed a guitar, and a violinist joined in and they broke into the novelty song from the mid-seventies.

Carly looked at Rose and Sandy. 'This is the world that I live in. Someone says something, and we all start singing a song. It's like Glee for adults, but much less dangerous than what I suspect Nic puts you through.'

The song stopped, and people began chatting about music stuff, the next Gympie Muster, and the show at Rockhampton. Rose sighed. 'It's not just a job, is it Carly? It's a way of life.'

'Yes, Rose, and once you get the bug, it's hard to get it out of your system. I used to work for the Brisbane City Council, and it bored me to tears. I was always angry, too, but I didn't know why. Then I met Sticks Out and gave it all up to do this. My parents keep hoping that I'll find a nice Accountant, settle down, pop out some rug-rats, and go all homely.'

Sandy smiled. 'Rose knows an Accountant. He's always looking for someone.'

'Is he married?'

'Yes, but it still doesn't stop him from looking. He's a creep.'

The group swapped the seating arrangement, and

Rose was alone with Nic in the Kombi Van. 'Sandy tells me Sticks Out has known you for years, but he won't give up any Nic Thorn secrets. There's something about a code of silence?'

'Yep, but now that you are alone with me, ask me any question. I'll be answering it with silence.'

'OK. Why haven't you made a play for Sandy? She really likes you.'

'Whoa, nope. Not going there. I know about your pact, Rose. Besides, 'We've got a groovy thing going.' Nic began singing the Simon and Garfunkel song from the '60s. 'Join in, Rose; the chorus is pretty simple.'

'No thanks. I'm just looking for a straight answer from you.'

'Nope, the best I can do is another Garfunkel song, 'The Sounds of Silence,' and again he sang, but Nic started mouthing words instead; no sound. 'They aren't any words, Rose. You guys are good for me. Everything is better, and I hope we can keep this going as long as possible. I've been doing these scam investigations for over ten years. Chewy and Driver are my only close friends; then you guys came down my long and winding road.'

'OK. Can we talk about something else, then? When are you going to be looking at something overseas? Surely the scams are going down everywhere?'

'Well, funny you mention that. If this goes well, there's something that involves live reptiles and bird smuggling. That's handled by the Queensland

Department of Fisheries and Ag, too. It might mean a trip to New Zealand or Fiji. Those countries were overseas last time I looked.'

'Good one, Nic-Bro. So that you know, my mother is from New Zealand. She made my Father pledge his allegiance to the All Blacks instead of the Wallabies as part of the wedding ceremony.'

Nic grinned and watched as the others in the Troopy overtook them. Crusoe was driving, Sticks Out was playing a paradiddle on the dashboard, and they were mid-song. Carly was in full voice, and Sandy was asleep in the back seat.

CHAPTER 12

They arrived at North Rockhampton and headed to the Cricket Ground, as this was the area set aside for the bands to play and stay. There were about fifty other vans and motorhomes parked in various spots. Nic and Crusoe stopped at their allocated sites. A stage was set up at one end of the oval, and three open-sided semi-trailers were on the flanks. They climbed out of the vehicles, stretched, and started setting up the annexe on the Troopy. Once that was done, Carly called the team together:

'This is where our day gigs are, but we also have two nights playing at The Great Western. That's where they put on the Rodeo Show too. Our show is more for the 'early to bedders', so we have the dinner and show set at six each night. Just letting you know that the cover charge is forty dollars, and twenty if you are a concession cardholder. It's only ten if you're with the Vets or Armed Services. Thanks to Nic for that further concession.' Carly then put his fist to her heart and tapped at it a few times.

Nic mock saluted, then added. 'No worries, Carly,

but there is something else as Rose, Sandy, and I might need to disappear after tonight's gig for a few hours. One of Rose's cousins has a cattle farm up north near Yamba and wants us to visit. We might be staying up there overnight. They'll pick us up, so we won't need to pull down the Troopy or take the Kombi.' Carly nodded. 'Thanks. Is there anything else we need to know? Will you be around for all the shows?'

'Nope, so that's the plan. I'm always on mobile if you need me in a hurry.' Crusoe spoke up. 'I can always cover you, Nic, if you're not around.'

Rose looked at him. 'But how will that work, Crusoe? You don't know how to play the songs.'

'I don't have to, Rose. I'll go all 'Marcel Marceau,' and mime it. I'll put tape on the neck of the guitar and pretend to strum. The backing track does the rest, even the vocals.'

'That's cheating, surely musicians don't do that sort of thing when playing live?'

Crusoe nodded. 'Yes, they do. Britney Speared got caught doing it in Las Vegas, and Mariah Canary has done it too, apparently, but they all call it *lip-syncing*. Then there was the duo 'Manilla Vanilla in the late eighties. Their whole show was other people singing.'

Rose shook her head. 'But surely they have people that check those things out?' Nic smiled, and Rose thought Carly was about to say something about him, so he quickly changed the subject. 'Where do we eat then?'

'Here, Rose. We get fifty per cent off any food and drink except alcohol. Any stall, any food. Just say 'I'm with the Band...''

'That's silly, Carly, anybody could say that.'

'Yes, but we musicians all know each other. So, anyone trying to use that gets closed down pretty quickly.' Rose began to move away. 'Good to know. Sandy and I are going off to get falafel burgers if any-one wants one?'

Sticks Out quipped quickly. 'Charred animal flesh all the way, for me baby.'

Nic laughed at Stick's comment. 'OK, guys. Our first show at the Great Western starts at six tonight, so make sure you're around at five to head off. That's in a couple of hours, and don't eat much either, as the nerves will start to kick in soon.'

Rose and Sandy headed for the "Vegie Vegan Vroom" stall and returned fifteen minutes later with their lunch. 'They wouldn't give us a discount as we forgot the name of our Band. We tried using Cilla Black and Cilla Presley, but that didn't work either. They told us Cilla Black was a redhead, then looked at Sandy and told us Cilla Presley wasn't a blonde. Shouldn't we be wearing wigs?'

'Yes, Rose, good point. I've organised the bouffant for the shows. Oh, and how do you guys feel about being a bride?'

'Err, why Carly? What has Nic told you?'

'Well, you guys did the backup singing theatrics so

well last time, so we have added it to the Great Western shows as part of the routine. Just do your thing from the start of that Julia Roberts movie, as they were all brides. Nic said you wouldn't mind.'

It was now 4:30 p.m., and as they were all getting a bit edgy, they decided to head to the venue. There was a shuttle bus for the ten-minute drive from the Cricket Ground, which also had a trailer for the music gear. Crusoe had gone over there earlier to check over the music desk so everything was ready for the performers to arrive.

At 5.45 p.m., the last duo, 'Cash and Co,' had moved off stage and 'The Dusty Spring Fields' were now setting up. Rose was on her own off-stage, dressed in the bridal outfit when a man approached her. He looked her over and smiled. 'Geez, I hope that dress has been used before, as you might not be allowed out of here if you're unmarried.'

'Thanks, I think, Mister....'

'Oh, it's..... you can call me Keith if you like.'

'Ok, thanks, Keith. Are you a singer, too?'

'Yes, I sing a little bit around the place, and good luck to you. It's a small crowd, only about a thousand or so. They pack them in a bit later when the headline act starts, with Lee, Troy, and John. I might be invited up to play something, too.'

'OK, well, good luck to you too, Keith. Here comes my friend Sandy. We're doing the bridal stuff for two songs for our band, 'The Dusty Spring Fields."

The man moved away, and Sandy approached Rose. 'Do you know who that was?'

Rose gave a wry smile. 'Nope. Keith someone. He said he sings and might get on stage if the three other blokes let him join in, but I think I know him from somewhere.'

Sandy was about to say something else, but Carly started singing. 'Son of a Preacher Man', followed up with 'The Look of Love', then 'You don't have to say you love me'. There was loud applause from the audience. Carly continued: *'Ok, these next two songs are just as well-known as those heartbreakers. Let us introduce the 'Cilla's, Cilla Black and Cilla Presley. They aren't their real names, folks...'*

Rose leaned into Sandy. 'That's the same thing she said at the Jazz Club. I wonder if Sticks Out will say his thing, too, when he introduces the Slim Dusty songs.'

Sandy agreed. 'I don't know, Rose, but we're up. Nic said don't look at the audience, as it might put you off. Oh, and despite what everyone says, don't imagine them naked.'

The audience appreciated their two songs and the theatrics for the second song, then the Cillas moved back off stage, and Sticks Out stood up just as the women predicted. 'My turn. This will be a little different as Nic, Carly, and I'll be doing harmonies and new arrangements with the Slim Dusty songs.......'.

The show finished at 7 p.m. The Dusty Springfield songs went down well, but the audience appreciated the new Slim Dusty arrangements. The Dusty Spring Fields thanked the audience and called Rose and Sandy onto the stage. Carly took to the microphone: 'Thank you, we have been to 'The Dusty Spring Fields' and will be back here tomorrow night, same time. We are also playing at the Cricket Oval across the river. Please come over and join us.'

The crowd cheered for an encore, but the troupe had already left the stage.

When they were gathered around backstage, Sticks Out spoke first. 'That was great, guys. I think the crowd was around fifteen hundred. It's up there with the biggest one I have done. I could get used to this.'

'Thanks, Sticks. It was the biggest one I've done for a while, too. But I know what you mean; I'd love Nic, Rose and Sandy with us at the Gympie Muster if we do that. Hey, is anyone staying around for Lee, Troy, and John? I think they come on at ten, and then Keith comes on after that. He might even perform with them, which would be great to watch.'

Rose called out from the stage dressing room. 'Hey, I was speaking to Keith before. He said the three other guys might not let him get up and play.'

Carly, Sticks, Crusoe and Nic all stopped what they were doing. 'You met Keith? Was Nicole with him too?' Rose shook her head. 'Is she his backup singer?'

Carly smiled. 'My God, Rose. So, it's true. You don't know anything about pop culture, music or movies?'

Rose grinned. 'Thanks, Carly, I think. Yes, movies and music are not quite my scenes.'

The group began grilling Rose for more details about Keith when a man approached them. He looked the part of a genuine cowboy, with cowboy swagger, spurs on his boots and chewing a matchstick. He was only about 1.5m tall and somewhat stocky. The Stetson was pressed firmly down on his head, bending his ears, and made them stick out. 'G'day. I'm looking for Nic Thorn. I'm C.T Driver.' Sticks flicked at his ears. 'Hi, I'm Sticks Out. You look like one of my cousins with those stick-out ears.'

'Nope, but, the surname is Driver. First name C.T.'

Sticks nodded. 'What does the C.T. stand for? Maybe you're a cousin?'

'Nope. Nic told me no first names.'

Nic held out his hand. 'Nice to meet you, C.T. Give us a bit and we'll be ready to come with you. These two, Rose and Sandy, will be coming with me as well.'

C.T. nodded. 'OK, mate. I didn't think it was the real Cilla Black and Cilla Presley on stage with you. Too young, but you never know these days with all that plastic surgery stuff you city folk are into. The rig is out the back when you are ready.'

'OK, but can you hang around a bit? Maybe grab a beer.'

C.T. looked at him. 'Nope. Sorry, mate. I don't touch that stuff. Bundaberg Sarsaparilla is my poison.'

Crusoe came over. 'You're good to go Nic. We can

take it from here. We'll see you tomorrow afternoon around two for the gig over the river, then?'

'Yep, thanks, Crusoe.'

Rose and Sandy had changed back into their civvies and moved towards C.T. Driver. 'Hey, Rose. Let's try and guess what the C.T. stands for. Nic will hate that.'

They moved off with Nic and C.T. Driver and went to the carpark, and Nic pointed them to the vehicle. It was a white Dual Cab Holden Commodore utility with high radio antennas at each corner and a massive bull bar. The front suspension had been lowered which made the car look like an angry white bull.

Rose looked at him. 'I thought you said it was a 'rig'? Charles Thomas, Colin Timothy, Cyril Todd...Are you going to tell us C.T., or do we have to keep guessing? How about it, Nic?'

Nic nodded. 'OK, this is the only time I'll permit you to know Driver's first name, just to keep you quiet.'

'Are you ready? ... C.T.'s initials are for....'

'Are you sure? Doesn't it breach all your security protocols?'

'Yep. I'm sure Rose...His name is ... 'Cattle Truck Driver. C.T Driver.'

C.T. looked at him sternly. 'Damn you, mate.'

The four climbed into the Dual Cab, headed south for Allentown, and then the half-hour drive onto Gracemere. It was now almost nightfall, and Rose noticed they were not heading north. 'Hey, we're heading south, Nic. Are we going in the right direction?'

'Yep, Rose, diversion and misdirection are my middle name.'

'Oh. I thought it was 'The'. You know like 'Winnie The Pooh', and 'Jack The Ripper'. Nic 'The' Thorn has a good ring to it.'

C.T. looked over to Nic. 'How long do I have to put up with these two, mate? I can drop them off anywhere. Another rig will be along in an hour or two.'

'Nope, but thanks for the offer. They are my team, and there is no 'I' in team.'

Rose sniffed the air. 'Where are we? It's the middle of nowhere. I can still smell cow, though. Is out here the true origin of the depletion of the ozone? Who knew?'

'No, Rose. It's 'Eau de Beef Lot,' and we are in the middle of it here, but we have excellent four-star accommodation at the Lilly Pilly Resort back in Gracemere tonight. There's a swimming pool and everything. We won't get to use it, though, as we're collecting the Cattle Truck first thing tomorrow and heading west.'

They stepped from the car, C.T. shut the door, locked the car, saluted and disappeared into the darkness. Sandy called out. 'So, where's he going? Walking back to Rockhampton?'

'No, Sandy, to his truck. He sleeps in it, but don't worry. He'll be back in the morning around five; then, we are going on a little road trip. I'll be in the truck with C.T., and one of you will drive the Dual Cab.'

'Five in the morning? Cripes.... that's up before the sparrows.'

'Yep, the early bird catches the worm, Rose.'

'Yes, Nic, but the second mouse gets the cheese.'

CHAPTER 13

Rose and Sandy were softly talking about the early morning rise when they were interrupted by a knocking at the internal adjoining door of their hotel room. 'Get up, guys as we leave in about fifteen minutes.'

Rose called back. 'It's only four-thirty, and you said five a.m. We still have another half hour of our beauty sleep.'

'Yep, and I said we're leaving at five, so you sleeping beauties must be up at four to make yourselves presentable to the herd of cows we're about to meet.' Rose opened the door, and Nic came into their room. The women were dressed, eating breakfast, drinking coffee, and packed, ready to leave.

'Where did you get the food? I planned on going to the BP Service Station on the way out of Gracemere.'

'It doesn't open until seven, so we planned ahead. What's on this morning that we must get up so early for then?'

Nic grabbed an apple, took a large bite, and offered it back to them; they both declined. 'OK, we're going west for a bit, then take a right into Malchi Nine Mile

Road. It's up near the racecourse, where we're meeting the crew from All Cattle Transporters.'

'How many are in the crew? Do we need to be concerned?'

'Nope. We're leaving you way back down the road. Do either of you know how to use a C.B. Radio?' Rose nodded. 'Roger, that roger.'

'We'll be on Channel 66, like Route 66, the U.S, Mother Road', and it'll be radio silence. Try and stay hidden, too.'

There was a sound of airbrakes in the street, and Nic nodded. 'That'll be C.T.' The group moved outside, and C.T. climbed down the steps from the truck. Rose looked the truck over. 'That is a nice rig, C.T.'

C.T. nodded. 'It's about twenty years old. I picked it up cheaply. It came with a trailer, too.' Sandy smiled. 'Why didn't you go newer? Nic likes his things all shiny and new.' C.T. continued: 'Trucks made before the year 2000 only require an electronic logging device unit, but after that, they need an Automatic On-Board Recording Device. This makes it easier to hide from the authorities as I can get away with just having a logbook. Ain't that right, mate?'

Nic took over. 'Yep, and the boss at the Trucking Company knows that this rig is not compliant, too, so it's our way in. The truck holds about a hundred cattle at three hundred per head. That's about thirty thousand per shipment.'

Rose looked towards the truck again, trying to work

out the numbers. 'So, what do they do? Round the cattle up, chuck them in C. T.'s truck, ship them to the market and take the money?' Nic nodded. 'Yep, that's about it, but they make a not-so-subtle adjustment to the ear tags before arrival.'

Sandy leaned forward. 'What? They change the numbers over with black Texta. I went with a guy once who used to change the licence plate on his Falcon with black paint to avoid speed cameras. The dope got fined for altering the plate.'

Nic leaned in and spoke a little quieter. 'No, they just cut the ears off, usually with shears, no anaesthetic.' C.T. nodded in confirmation, and Nic continued: 'OK, guys let's roll. Stay on the channel, radio silence. Keep your speed under sixty as this old bus isn't built for speed. Watch for the right-hand turn, and stop and wait, when we get to a rise. We'll be driving for about six kilometres.'

Nic climbed up, C.T. went to the other side, and they chugged off down the highway. Rose followed them in the Dual Cab and kept well behind them as instructed, going west along the Capricorn Highway. Rose could see that the truck was slowing to make a right-hand turn into the road, so she slowed the car down to maintain the distance. 'How long do we keep following them?'

'Nic said the Racecourse is about six kilometres in. How about we use the trip meter?' Sandy then took a breath. 'Are you scared, Rose?'

'Yes. It might get too much one day, and our waxed wings will melt in the sun. Hopefully not out here though, as I haven't seen another car or a homestead.'

'Me either.'

Meantime, in the Cattle Truck, C.T. looked over to Nic. 'How ugly do you think this could get, mate? I don't think the Boss is on to me yet as I'm just another one of his flunky drivers. I've heard that he churns them over quickly before they ask too many questions.' C.T. started changing down through the gears. 'How are we going to do this? I mean, what's the cover? Who are you, and why are you with me this morning?'

Nic nodded. 'I've been thinking about that. How do you feel about me being your new friend? You know that you picked up at the Rockhampton Show?'

C.T. looked over, taking his eyes from the road. 'What's that supposed to mean? Oh, no, Nic, I'm not going all 'Brokeback Mountain', no way.'

Nic laughed. 'No, let's leave it as a friend visiting from Brisbane. Let's use the 'Rose's cousin' story.' C.T. nodded. 'That will work, mate.'

C.T. went through the Racetrack gates and trundled around the back to the cattle yards. There was a group of men standing around. 'That's the Boss there. He calls himself Vince. It looks like his sixteen-year-old son is here too, Vince Junior; call him Junior. He's a big boy for his age, and we'll have to watch him, but.

He wants to impress his dad all the time with tough talk. The other two blokes I haven't seen before.'

'Good, four against four if needed.'

'We are only two.'

'Yep, but Rose and Sandy are in the Dual Cab.'

'You're kidding, mate. How can they help? They're about six kilometres away.'

'Good point, but they haven't followed us in here, so most likely are sitting atop a hill with eyes on us. By the way, C.T., is there a gun in the truck somewhere?'

'Yes, there's a locked rifle box under the seats in the cabin. Do you want it?'

'Nope, just checking. Fists and kicks we can take, but guns with bullets tend to make it something more permanent.'

C.T. sighed heavily. 'So mate, are you expecting trouble?'

'No idea, the Department of Ag tells me it's been going on for months, and they reckon it could be over three hundred thousand dollars so far, and that's a lot of bull to give up. It might just be a recon this morning as there aren't any cattle.'

C.T. brought the truck to a stop, and they climbed down.

'Hey Boss, what's the early call for? By the way, this is Nic. He's me mate from one of the bands at the Rockhampton Rodeo Show. I'm just showing him a bit of country life.'

The Boss-man nodded, then pointed towards the

others. 'This is my son, Vince Junior, and these two are Bill and Ben.' The group shook hands and Vince Junior nodded.

Nic looked at the older man. 'Thank you so much for letting me come along too, but I won't be much help as I don't like to get all muddy and dusty, and I don't like the smell.'

Junior looked at Nic, then spat on the ground. 'Looks like we've got a ripe one here, Dad. How about we get him in the back of the truck? I can prod him a few times with my cattle persuader.'

The lad revealed a two-pronged cattle prod from behind his back. It was about seventy centimetres long. He pulled the trigger, and a blue charge lit and crackled across the tines.

Vince looked over at the lad and smiled. 'Not today son. We're bringing the herd down tomorrow—same time. I just wanted to know if everyone was good for it. You can come too, Nic, but keep out of our way.' The group of men all nodded.

C.T. looked at his boss. 'How many cattle am I moving? And where are they going to, Boss?'

Vince glared at him. 'No questions, no answers. You know the drill. Ask too many questions, and you might not like the answers. You'll only drive for me this one time, and I'm already having a bad feeling about you.'

C.T. nodded, and Junior smiled, then he hefted the cattle prod between his hands. 'Just say the word,

Dad. I'd love to see a man's eyes bug out after a few jabs with this little beauty.'

C.T. nodded again. 'Well understood, Boss. See you here tomorrow then.' Vince narrowed his eyes and glared at them. 'Just be on time.'

Nic and C.T. climbed back into the cattle truck and left the site. They collected Sandy and Rose along the way, and all met up at the BP on the outskirts of Gracemere. It had just opened for business, so the group found a table. Rose took Sandy to get breakfast. C.T. took the opportunity to lean towards Nic. 'I don't like where this is going, mate. Do we have a backup plan?'

'I'm working on it. The Stock and Rural Crime Investigations Squad are around but can't get involved yet, but I have something in mind.'

Rose and Sandy came back, and Nic went through the latest development. 'It's on for tomorrow morning, so we need to return here. Are you guys good for that? Just watch out for Vince Junior. He's carrying a cattle prodder and likes to prod the people and shock the cows.'

Sandy nodded, but Rose shook her head. 'Sorry Nic, I'll have to stand out. After the show, I'd like to catch up with my cousin and her family. It will probably be a late night, so I won't be much good for you at five in the morning.'

Nic nodded. 'OK, I'll use Carly, and see what I can

find out about Bill and Ben.' Sandy laughed. 'Check the flowerpots.'

'Funny, Sandy, so let's get back to Rockhampton. We have about four hours to prepare for the afternoon show, and we're on again tonight at the Rodeo.'

The group said their goodbyes to C.T. and drove back to Rockhampton.

CHAPTER 14

At 2 p.m., 'The Dusty Spring Fields' were playing their gig on the back of the open truck at the Cricket Oval and readied themselves for the evening event. Rose noticed the same script was being used, 'Hey, Sandy. Carly said the same things here again today. It's like everything is rehearsed, not just the music.'

Sandy smiled. 'Yes, Rose, it's all about timing and maintaining the consistent sound for the show. Saying things ad-lib could mean a need to change the microphone settings, that sort of thing.'

Rose nodded. 'By the way, I googled Keith. He is one of the biggest country music stars in the world at the moment. Not bad for a guy from Caboolture.' Sandy looked at Rose. 'Actually, he was born in New Zealand, but we claim him as an Aussie, just like Russell Crowe, Phar Lap and the pavlova.'

The evening gig went well, but this time, Rose forgot to swap over her Rossi Boots for the wedding shoes, and this brought up a greater cheer when they went through the routine. Rose met up with her cousins and called back to the others. 'Don't wait up. I'd like to try sleeping in their Winnebago. It's the big grey one at the caravan park. It has hot showers, electric blankets and everything.'

Carly, Sandy, and the boys hung around for the next couple of shows and left halfway through the John Williamson gig. Crusoe had gone off to look at the sound desk being operated for the current performance, so Nic called the others together for an update: 'We have an early start again. C.T. will be meeting us at the Racecourse. Sandy and Carly, I'll get you to wait for us at the Lilly Pilly Hotel in Gracemere – out of sight. The service station won't be open, and I don't want Vince thinking I've brought along someone to get in the way.'

Sticks looked over to Nic. 'Do you need me then?'

'Nope. Stay here and help Crusoe get ready for tomorrow's show.'

The group left the Rodeo Show and caught the shuttle bus back to their camp.

At 4 a.m. the next morning, Nic collected Sandy and Carly and they drove to the BP Service Station at Gracemere. He dropped them off, then headed to the racecourse. About halfway along the road, he came up to a herd of cattle being led through a farm gate. Nic noticed Junior was walking at the rear whilst Bill and Ben were on horseback. Vince was not around, so he assumed he was with C.T. waiting for them. Nic patiently stayed behind the herd as they were led into the cattle yards, and he noticed C.T. and Vince already there.

C.T. saw Nic and came over. 'This is the plan, mate. They steal the cattle and cut their tags off in transit. I drive the cattle to the Feed Lot, take the cash and give it to Vince. What a scam. It's all on the truck driver if we get caught.'

'So, what happens here? Just the loading? Where do they cut the ear tags off?'

'The cattle can't move much in the trailers, mate, so Bill, Ben and Junior are doing the nasty bit whilst I drive the truck to the Feed Lot. The ear tags get chucked on the side of the road for the crows to munch on. I can't see the point, though, as the plastic ear tags wouldn't deteriorate that quickly. I assume they don't expect anyone to find them anyway, there's nothing out this way apart from the bulldust. I've been told to take the A3 towards Bouldercombe. They'll bang on the chassis roof when I am to stop and let them out. Job done. Vince collects the crew and then tells me where the Feed Lot is.'

'Any stops?'

'Well, no mate, but I've told Vince I've forgotten to fill the fuel tank so we have to stop at the BP Gracemere. We won't be there long, and Junior has already threatened to jab me with the cattle prod if I try anything stupid.'

Nic whispered. 'So that's where we will make our

play. I'll make a call to set up things with the Department of Ag.'

C.T. nodded. 'No worries mate, but don't get caught making the call. They insist on radio silence, and that means phones too.'

'OK, I'll use text. Thanks for the tip.'

Nic returned from sending the message, and Junior approached him brandishing the cattle prod. 'Morning Nic. I keep forgetting to keep this charged up. You never know when something will have a go at you. One of them did this to me.'

The young man removed his driza-bone and had a T-shirt on underneath.

Nic saw a row of stitches from the top of his arm to his wrist. 'Thirty-eight stitches here. The stupid bull wanted to put its stupid horn into me. I got him back with my electric jabber here, and he didn't look so well after that. I don't think his eyes have ever stopped spinning.'

Nic grimaced. 'Good to know, Junior. So, what's this early morning cattle thing about, then? I thought you only had to get up early for the milking cows. When are these going to be milked?'

'Are you for real? These are for meat. Don't you know the difference?'

'Nope, I don't know anything about farming stuff. This is my first time out of the city. I just play music. Both kinds...country and western.'

'You're a real drongo.' Junior walked off laughing,

and then C.T. came over. 'What was that all about? What did you say?'

'Nothing much. Hopefully, he thinks I'm not a threat no matter what happens.'

Junior, Bill, and Ben then guided the cattle into the truck, and Vince just stood around watching everything. C.T. and Nic were now waiting in the truck's cab, and Nic had given Bill the keys to drive the Dual Cab back to Gracemere.

C.T. wound up the truck window and stretched. 'They aren't happy about me stopping in Gracemere, mate, but I can't go anywhere without knowing how much fuel I need to have.'

'Yep. Just make sure you drive slowly and re-fuel as slowly as you can. I just got a response back from the Department of Ag that they are on the other side of Rockhampton and they might not be there when we arrive.'

'OK, that's not good but, but OK.' Nic and C.T. jumped when Junior thumped on the cab's roof to let them know the cattle were loaded and ready to travel. C.T. started the engine, and Nic noticed the others hadn't moved.

C.T. then received a text: *No funny stuff, C.T. Take your money today and go.*

Another text came through a couple of minutes later: *No more than half a tank required.* He showed it to Nic. 'Mate, this means I won't have far to go, but once I get there, I won't come back this way. I have a bad feeling about this.'

About forty-five minutes later, they'd arrived at the service station. C.T. pulled the truck to a stop, and Junior called out from the trailer. 'Dad's just rung me. It looks like you are not who you say you are, so Nic, you do the re-fuelling. We're climbing out, so don't move.'

C.T. climbed down from the truck's cab, stood by the truck and handed Nic his Credit Card to pay for the fuel. The BP was not yet fully open, so it was credit card self-service only at the diesel pump. Vince drove up, and then Nic's phone started ringing.

Meantime, Junior had climbed out of the trailer along with Ben, and shook the cattle prodder at Nic 'Don't answer that. Remember, radio silence.' C.T. looked at Nic. 'Sorry mate, they must've found something about me.'

Vince came up to them. 'So, you're not 'just' a truck driver, are you? I get that people have a history they like to keep on the down low, but why would an ex-S.A.S. Officer be interested in driving my cattle? I admit I needed a driver more than I needed to check you out, but that's on you, not me. Junior, take him down, and use the prodder.'

Nic noticed the smirk on Junior's face. 'You really don't want to do that, Junior.'

Junior sniggered. 'OK, Nic. You can shut up too. If

Dad wants me to take your little friend down. It's what I'll have to do. He's the Boss.'

This time C.T. looked at him. 'Don't. It may hurt you more than it will hurt me.' Vince laughed, looked over and nodded to Ben. 'We are four against two, C.T.' Junior held the cattle prod like a sword and swooshed it in the air. 'This is going to be like real fun, Dad. Most times you want me to stop. Do I have your permission to keep going this time?'

'Yep, go your hardest; make it stunning.' Vince laughed at his comment. Junior stepped forward, pressed the trigger and the prodder arced. 'I've always wanted to take on the S.A.S.'

C.T. stood motionless, with his arms crossed over his chest. 'Please put it down, Junior, and let's talk about this, mate.'

Junior came at C.T. with a parry, and he fended it off. The lad smiled. 'You know, *mate*, these prongs are supposed to snap off if you push them too hard into the animal, but I fixed that with super-glue. It like makes the bulls pretty cranky. Are you going to like get all angry with me then?'

Vince noticed that Nic hadn't moved either. 'Hey, Nic. Have you seen what a cattle prod does to a man?'

Nic lowered his head. 'No, I haven't, Vince. Could you ask your son not to do this, please? It's not very ...nice. It might hurt him.'

C.T. moved a little closer to the truck door and a

step closer to Junior. Nic realised that he was giving himself an option for the next stage of the challenge.

Junior thrust the cattle prod directly towards his face, so C.T. clapped his hands together, and the wand stopped inches from his head. Junior pressed the trigger again and the blue charges arced angrily across the tines.

'You can't stop this.' Junior forcibly twisted the prodder from C.T.'s grip.

C.T. shook his head. 'Don't do this, Junior. It's your last chance, mate.'

Junior laughed and again thrust the cattle prod towards C.T., however this time, C.T. suddenly ducked his head out of the way, which meant Junior was propelled forward into the door of the truck chassis. It was metal against the electric charge, the metal bit back and shorted out. The electric charge skipped up the shaft and bounced into Junior's chest. He went down with a shriek.

Vince looked down at him, quivering on the ground. 'Damn you kid, that was stupid. Ben, bring the gun from my Ute, will you?'

Ben brought the rifle over, pointed it towards Nic and C.T. and told them to turn around. He bound their wrists with plastic ties and sat them down against the truck wheels with their hands clasped behind their backs.

Vince glared at them now, looked around, and then smiled as he realised it was still too early for any witnesses or interruptions. 'OK, you two. Again, why is an ex-S.A.S. Officer interested in my little cattle duffing charade?'

Nic and C.T. just sat there. 'Ben, which one do you reckon will break first? I think Nic here is a big softy, so give him a little chin music and see what happens.'

Ben helped Nic to stand and then punched him in the stomach. Nic sucked in a few deep breaths but remained standing. 'Gee, Ben. Is that all you've got?'

Vince then took the rifle from Ben, unloaded it, held it by the barrel and swung it a few times as if holding a baseball bat. 'So which shoulder? Are you right or left-handed?'

Nic shook his head. 'Both, Vince. I'm a guitarist and have a gig in a few hours.'

Vince moved up to Nic, pulled down the shoulders of his windbreaker, and then swung the stock of the gun into the top half of Nic's right arm. The smacking sound of wood against flesh split the morning silence. He then swapped hands and swung it again into Nic's left side bicep.

'You might not be playing your gig this arvo. Had enough yet, smart guy?'

Nic showed no emotion. 'It's merely a flesh wound, Vince. Take these cuffs off so I can rub my arms, please. Was it supposed to hurt?'

Vince glared at him, then looked down at Junior, who was still out of it. 'Just point the damn gun at them, Ben, and what the hell has happened to Bill?'

Vince then directed Ben to strike C.T. across the head with the gun barrel, but fortunately, as C.T. saw it coming, it was just a glancing blow. Although, his head snapped back with the connection, and blood began dribbling from the wound. Vince glared down at him again. 'OK, Mr S.A.S., Ben will put the bullets back in now - it might hurt a little less, but this time you won't wake up.'

Ben loaded the gun.

Vince smiled again, 'OK, have it your way then. Take your aim, Ben.' Vince grinned. 'There's no one around, so you can call for help if you want to.'

Ben cocked the gun and aimed it at C.T.

C.T. took a deep breath, then looked over to Nic. 'Have you got an aspirin, mate? I think I'm coming down with a headache. I could be the death of me.' C.T. laughed at his statement.

Nic smiled. 'Sorry, I can't help. I'm a bit tied up.'

A throbbing engine noise broke the silence as a large black Harley Davidson Sport Glide appeared through the early morning fog. As it came closer, the rider stopped, and the stand was kicked down. The biker stepped off, removed the helmet and a long plait of grey hair cascaded from beneath. He stopped in front of the group. 'Looks like you've caught a couple of ripe ones there, mate.'

Nic looked up. 'Yep, I know but I have it all under control.'

Vince laughed again. 'Who is this? Another one

of your backup singers?' The biker took another look around, climbed back on his ride and headed off into the darkness.

C.T. watched him go. 'I hope he wasn't the backup, Nic.'

Nic looked over at him. 'Nope,' then suddenly the group was bathed in the headlight glare from a half-circle of Harley-Davidsons. 'But they might be.'

Vince raised his hand to shield himself from the bright lights. 'What's going on?'

Nic took a breath. 'As I just said, I have it all under control.'

The biker returned to the group holding up an official badge, and he had a couple of his burly mates with him, along with Sandy and Carly.

'It's over now, Vince.'

Vince stared at him. 'Damn it. This was my last one too.'

Ben sighed heavily. 'You had to go one more time didn't you, Boss? I told you they were onto us. I told you that C.T. was bad news, but no, you're never wrong.'

'Shut up Ben. I'm trying to think.'

Vince stood there contemplating his next move when Sandy moved forward, helped Nic to rise, and severed the plastic ties with a knife, then she squatted down next to C.T. and did the same.

Nic began to wring his hands together, trying to alleviate the pain in his upper arms from the attack.

'I don't think I can play the gig this arvo. It looks like Crusoe might get his chance after all. Bring on the mime.'

Vince glared at Ben. 'Next time, just don't tell me I'm wrong. Do something about it.' Vince sighed, conceded defeat, and indicated to Ben to lower the gun.

The Rural Inspection officer approached them again and softly shook Nic and C.T.'s hands. 'Thanks, guys, this one had been tricky to catch in the act. We've been chasing it for months. One of the farmers along the highway noticed the ear tags and stored them for us. After a bucket or two, he called us in to have a look.'

He then looked over at Vince. 'And on behalf of the Department of Agriculture and Queensland Police, Vincent Ernest Reilly, I am authorised, as a Rural Inspections Officer, to place you under arrest. Charges include stealing cattle and committing aggravated acts of cruelty to animals. We already have Bill Crusie in custody.' The officer then looked down at the youth crumpled on the ground. 'And once your boy wakes up and stops dribbling, he'll be arrested too.'

Carly approached Nic and softly rubbed his biceps. C.T. looked over at them. 'Hey, guys. I've got a nasty bump on the head.' Nic leaned over and kissed him on the forehead.

Blue flashing lights from an incoming Police wagon illuminated the pink sunrise and stopped in the carpark. The First Aid kit from the service station was brought over to attend to C.T.'s head wound, but nothing much could be done for Nic, so he popped a couple of aspirin for the pain.

Nic's group was standing over Vince Junior, each suggesting ways to wake him up. Sandy and Carly eventually squatted down to massage his legs and arms. He slowly woke up and stared at them. 'My eyes won't stop spinning.'

CHAPTER 15

The Police loaded Vince, Junior, Bill and Ben into the Police wagons and they drove off. Nic's group then went inside the service station for breakfast, and the Rural Inspection officer formally introduced himself. 'I'm Eddie. Sorry about the coming in after the punch in the guts, Nic. I had to wait until I knew the Police van was almost here.'

Nic nodded. 'No worries. It takes the focus off the pain in my arms anyway. You guys did well to stay out of sight.'

Eddie nodded. 'Well, we'd been here since four a.m. waiting and watching.'

Carly and Sandy returned with coffee orders, and Nic took a sip of his chai tea. Carly moved up to Nic. 'So, you're definitely out for this arvo's gig then?'

Nic grimaced at the pain. 'Yep, even if I can get my arms working, I won't be much good for the whole hour. I don't think I can do any dancing either.'

Carly nodded. 'I'll give Sticks Out and Crusoe the heads up on returning to Rockhampton. Have we finished down here?'

'Yep. Eddie's team will tidy up the cattle stuff, and return the herd to the owners, and then, they'll head down to the Feed Lot and conduct a few investigations there.'

C.T. looked at Nic. 'When are you guys heading back down to Brisbane?'

'Leaving tomorrow arvo. Carly and her band 'The Sweetened Plums,' have a gig at the Jazz Club in a few days. The life of a real musician never wanes.'

Another one of the Veteran Motorcycle Club members came over. He was dressed in full regalia, had a long beard, and a Vet bandana. Nic stood to greet him, and they moved away for privacy. 'Nic Thorn, it's been too long, buddy. What's it been about eight years?'

'About that long, Maxie. We were doing beer yards at the Breakfast Creek Hotel the last time I saw you. You told me that you had dumped the job, dumped the house, dumped the wife, and bought a one-way ticket to the Whitsunday Islands. How did that work out?'

'Well, I got as far as Airlie Beach and met the Vets Motorcycle Club up there. Their leader punched the big ticket, and I bought his Fat Boy. I've been chasing the long white line ever since, mate, and I love it. Living the life of the eternal 'Easy Rider,' Nic. I help out Eddie occasionally whenever he gives us a hoi.'

They bumped fists, and Nic nodded. 'Thanks for coming down from Rockhampton this morning. We didn't know where this cattle duffing thing was headed.' Maxie nodded. 'So Nic, them women, Carly, Sandy and Rose, the backup singers, Are they your women?'

Nic smiled. 'Not quite, they both work with me on these investigations, and it still has its moments of excitement. I met Rose and Sandy about a year ago, and they have made the darkness of my job a little lighter.'

They hugged, back slapped, and Maxie twirled his finger. The rest of the Veterans rose from their breakfast tables, exited the service station and the throbbing of thirty Harley-Davidsons interrupted the morning serenity.

Carly then stood up. 'OK, I think we had better make tracks, too. We have about four hours before our gig to get Crusoe up to speed. I can see if we can push our show back an hour. It shouldn't be a problem as I know the guys in the band coming on after us. I'll get them to swap over. Everyone good to go?'

Sandy called out. 'Yes, I've even got my whip ready to flog the drivers on the way back.'

Carly laughed. 'I was wondering what you were going to do with it.'

'I could always use it on Nic if he gets out of line.' They said their goodbyes to Eddie and C.T. and joined the biker convoy for the drive back to Rockhampton.

A couple of hours later Nic and Rose were driving along the main street after having lunch. 'How were your cousins?' Rose smiled. 'It was interesting. We spent most of the time talking about how my Father runs his businesses and my Mother's contempt for anyone who doesn't measure up. My cousins knew about you, too. They told me that Mother likes you and sees you as a prospective son-in-law, but my Father thinks you're not worthy.'

'Good to know, at least I have something to work on.'

'What's that? The son-in-law part?'

'No, being worthy.'

Rose shook her head. 'I think you'll have to work hard.'

They drove into the Cricket Ground and Carly approached them. 'Sorry, guys. We're on in fifteen minutes. I forgot the other Band had already gone back to Brisbane. I don't want to bail. Are you guys good to go?'

Nic nodded. 'Yes, we're both in fine voice. We've been singing Christmas Carols in the Rockhampton mall, for lunch money. What about Sandy and Crusoe?' Carly nodded. 'They're already backstage. We've been wondering why you guys were taking so long.' Rose sighed. 'I'm driving my cousin's Prius. It shakes a bit going over thirty kilometres an hour.'

Rose went over to the backstage area where Sandy was already dressed as a bride but the wig was currently on the ground, and she was stomping on it. 'I think bugs are living in it, and it makes my head itchy.'

Rose nodded. 'OK. We'll do the wedding dresses. No wigs.'

Nic came up with Crusoe. 'It's his first time singing, guys; please go easy on him.' Sandy smiled. 'Sure, but this is only our fourth time. Besides, you said he would be miming.'

'Yep, there is that.'

Carly and the band started up. The sound was the same, even the same vocal commentary from Carly came through the audio speakers. When they got to the part about introducing the Cillas, Carly wasn't quite ready as the narration began: *OK, these following two songs are just as well-known as those heartbreakers....* Carly sheepishly looked over to Rose and Sandy waiting in the wings and mouthed, ' Oops...'

Rose and Sandy came from stage left, and Nic came from stage right. He nodded at them and smiled. He was dressed as a groom, Top Hat, and Tails, including a sprig of barley in his buttonhole. They all shared their microphone, and Nic helped them with the theatrical actions from the opening scene of 'My Best Friend's Wedding.'

The crowd were in rapture.

The two songs finished, and the women curtseyed. Nic bowed, and they began to walk off stage. He'd managed to raise his arms to guide Rose and Sandy, when someone in the crowd yelled, ' Hey, you're a big-a-mist.'

Nic stopped, turned, and yelled back. 'Yep, having multiple wives is legal in some states of America, but unfortunately, we're in Rockhampton.'

The crowd cheered again.

Sticks Out then stood up from behind the drums, *'My turn, guys, this is going to be a little different....'* Rose whispered to Nic. 'Is Crusoe supposed to be singing and playing the guitar? I think people are beginning to notice.'

'Not sure, but he's doing a good job with the guitar, isn't he?'

'Nic, the guitar is not plugged into the audio system, and I think Carly just turned off his microphone.' Nic nodded. 'Yep, I noticed that too.'

'The Dusty Spring Fields' completed their last song with a rambunctious version of Waltzing Matilda. Nic, Sandy and Rose had joined them on stage. The group linked their arms and went round and round on the scene until the music faded. The crowd were up on their feet and calling out for more.

This time, the Band decided to comply with an impromptu acapella version of 'The Carnival is Over.' This was 'The Seekers' classic farewell song. Sandy knew all the words so she led the group.

Meantime, Rose googled the song on her iPad so she could catch up and when it finished, they bowed, and Carly thanked them for their resounding applause: 'Thank you, and until next time, we have been 'The

Dusty Spring Fields' with special guests Cilla Black, Cilla Presley and the very, Mr Hansome, our groom.'

The group waved, exited and backstage, they congratulated themselves on the performances. Nic looked at Rose and Sandy. 'Guys, that was great. If my arms were working, I'd hug you both, so how about I give you a tip instead? Take an umbrella when it rains.'

Rose shook her head. 'Thanks for that, but will we get paid for this one?'

'Well, after deducting the fee for the sound desk hire, campsite hire, fuel, rental on the vehicles, meals and other expenses, nothing is left to divvy up.'

Rose shook her head in dismay.

A while later, the group were sitting around a campfire when Rose suddenly stood up. 'Sorry, guys, I've just remembered I have to get the Prius back to the Caravan Park.' Sandy looked at her. 'It's after nine, Rose. I suggest you want another night in the five-star Winnebago.'

Rose stopped. 'Well, there is that. But I can't let a double bed go to waste, can I? And the lovely hot shower, the space, and the comfy chairs, and the list goes on.'

Nic laughed. 'True, so see you in the morning at about nine, at the Western Rodeo. We have the photo shoot that you promised Maxie and his crew.'

Rose couldn't scamper away quickly enough, and the others retired for the night.

In the morning, they packed up the annexe, loaded the last of the music gear into the vehicles, and headed over the river to meet Rose and Maxie for the photos. Nic had arranged for one of the photographers to attend from the local Rockhampton daily paper, 'The Morning Bulletin.' Rose and Sandy wore the wedding dresses, and they tried to tempt Nic into putting on the top hat and tails, but he wasn't interested.

'Hey, guys. I wouldn't put it past you to have a pastor around here somewhere, and somehow, I end up married. To *both* of you.'

The photographer had them sitting on top of the rails looking at the rodeo ring, and then a couple of the Bikers drove their Harleys around in circles, providing the swirling dust. Brunch was now being served, and Maxie and Nic had purchased a Chiko Roll, the Australian version of the deep-fried spring roll on steroids. Maxie took one bite and then smiled at Nic, googled something on his phone, and held it up to show him. 'So, what d'ya reckon? Can I have one more photo shoot?' Nic shrugged. 'I don't think so, but you'll have to ask them. Don't be surprised if they say no.'

Maxie stood up and went over to one of his colleagues. The man jogged off, and moments later, a Harley Davidson FXS Shovelhead was ridden into the arena. Rose and Sandy looked up as Maxie approached them. 'One more shoot, please, ladies.' Neither knew what it was all about, however, Carly had been passing by Nic and Eddie when she overheard the mention of the 'The Chiko Roll poster,' so she googled it and showed it to Rose and Sandy.

Rose shook her head. 'No way, besides the motorcycle in the original poster was a Triumph, not a Harley.'

The photographer set up a green Backdrop screen and portable lighting whilst the Harley was rolled to a stop in front of the screen. Rose and Sandy were directed to sit on the bike, still in the wedding dresses, with the bikers in a semi-circle behind them. The photographer told the group it would be on the front page tomorrow with the headline: *'Look what rode down the road at the Rockhampton Rodeo.'*

Rose and Sandy eventually moved away from the shoot and found Nic and Carly. 'Are we good to go now? Sandy has just turned down her sixteenth proposal.'

About an hour later, the bikers left, and Nic's crew went to the vehicles to head back to Brisbane. It was another convoy. Rose, Sandy and Carly were again in the Kombi, and the men in the Troopy.

Just as they were nearing Brisbane, Sandy's phone rang. 'Oh Hi, sure. Tomorrow would be fine—eleven o'clock at 'The Coffee Club,' Eagle Street Pier. Thanks. Looking forward to catching up with you.'

'Who was that, Sandy? You didn't sound sure that you wanted to meet him.'

'It was her, Rose. Do you remember Alexandra

Ripley from school? She found me on Facebook and wants to meet up. Something about a school reunion in a few months: I was surprised she didn't want you to come with me. I'll go and see what it's all about.'

It was dusk when they finally arrived home. Carly dropped them off, and Dog greeted them. He was insisting on being fed, at least with a pre-dinner snack. Pucker came out to greet them. 'Hey, I've just fed Dog, so don't take any crap from him. He eats more than my Ice Hockey Team, and there are eleven of them.'

CHAPTER 16

Sandy and Pucker moved inside, and Rose was standing on the kerb with the luggage, when Dave ambled over from next door, still on crutches. 'Hey, Rose. Pucker's done well to tame that beast of yours. It only managed to scare the Postman twice. Has she told you about Dog and the nose-kissing thing yet?'

'Not yet. But how are you feeling? Still on the Vicodin?'

'No, just Panadol. I'm driving now, too. Just to the shops and back, though. It's never a good experience when you try to save a damsel in distress, let alone their car. I won't do that again. Did Nic find out any more about why it was taken?'

'Yes. It turns out someone transferred the car over to their name and used it as security, then they defaulted on the loan, and that's why the Repo Agent came.'

Dave was surprised it was that easy. 'I've never heard of that happening. So, they just got the Vehicle Identification Number from the car, and the banks don't bother to check? There must be more to it than that, Rose.'

'There is. Sandy lost her handbag about twelve months ago. It contained her driver's license and Credit Card, and someone had used her ID to take out loans. They even managed to take a mortgage out against her house. Nic is still getting that sorted.'

Dave nodded. 'Nic's been good for you two, hasn't he? Still, it must have its challenges given his background.'

'It has, but what's in Nic's background that we should know about?'

'Whoa, OK. Didn't he tell you? Nic was.....Well, he was dishonourably discharged from the Australian Federal Police. I only know because your Uncle Albert wanted to use Nic's services for something and did a Probity check. Sorry, I thought you guys knew?'

Rose shook her head. 'It's never come up. I did wonder how Nic gets the leads on the scams and things he investigates. I don't think Sandy knows about it either.'

Dave continued: 'Well, not unless Albert told her on his death bed or Nic had him swear to secrecy. Albert only told me about it while working through his funeral attendance list. That was sad, knowing he was about to die. He called one day from the hospital, and I answered Sandy's phone. She'd gone for a walk, and I was outside painting her back deck. The telephone reception from the hospital was pretty lousy, and I tried to explain that I wasn't Sandy, but he kept talking anyway. He loved you two guys so much. He had almost given up on everything years before, then he got together with you guys and opened 'The She Shed.' It made him feel important.'

'Thanks, Dave. We still miss him. And so, our Nic does have a skeleton in his cupboard, after all. I wonder if he was invited to the funeral then. He didn't say anything about it when he came with me.'

Dave nodded. 'It's our secret. Don't tell him I told you. I heard you ask him a few months ago if he killed people. I didn't hear his reply, though.'

Rose laughed. 'Nope. It's not his scene. He uses his resources and respects the law. I don't doubt he knows people that would if he asked nicely them to do so.'

'Thanks, I think.'

Dave hobbled off home, and Rose brought the luggage into the house, dropping hers in her room and leaving Sandy's by her bedroom door. She was going to the lounge room when she heard a shriek from Pucker. 'Look, he's doing it again, Sandy. I slept on the sofa bed, and that damn cat jumped onto my chest, then comes to my face and kisses my nose. It's so gross.'

Sandy was still laughing when Rose entered the room to see what all the fuss was about. Dog was sitting on Pucker's chest, licking her nose. Rose grinned. 'So now you know what it's like to be kissed constantly, Pucker. Some people don't like you kissing them either.'

'No way, I've never had any complaints. Anyway, I need to get going, I have an Ice Hockey practice session tonight at Boondall. Dave was good fun. Happy to house-sit for you guys anytime, it gives me a break from my hubby.' Pucker stood up and Dog dropped to the floor, he swiped his paw at her leg to let her know he was happy about it.

Rose looked at Pucker. 'I didn't know you were married.'

'It's all good. It's been nearly twenty-five years. He was the first one to call me Pucker. I think he's forgotten my name is Pauline.' She hugged them and approached the front door. 'And get that man of yours back down to the Ice Arena again. I would love to see what he can do on a pair of ice skates, especially with some of that 'Bolero' music playing in the background.'

'Who are you talking to, Pucker? Dog, me or Sandy? Nic isn't our man.'

'Oh, sorry, I didn't realise. I thought he was with both of you. There is so much of that honey to go around.' They waved her off and Sandy called out: 'See ya next time, Pucker. Dog is missing kissing you already.'

Rose then went to the kitchen to rustle up some dinner, opened the fridge and noticed a plastic storage container with a sticky note attached: *Enjoy. It's*

Pucker Tucker Time.' Rose lifted it out and showed it to Sandy.

'I saw that too. There are more frozen dinners in the freezer, too. Pucker got bored, so she cooked up a batch of veggie lasagne and moussaka for us. She still says we're too skinny.'

'Did you tell her about Rockhampton and the Chiko Roll thing?' Sandy smiled. 'I did, but she was more interested in whether the Chiko Rolls tasted the same after all these years.'

Rose nodded. 'You know, I didn't realise she was married. So many people have so many secrets, don't they? Tell me about this woman you're meeting to-morrow. I don't remember an Alexandra at St Marga-ret's school.'

'Me either, but it may not be the primary school where you and I met. I did Year One, Two and Three at West End. Maybe it was at that school, but a school reunion? That would make you around five or six years old. It could be a twenty-five-year thing. You're over thirty now.'

'Thanks for reminding me. I feel so old around you.'

Rose smiled. 'Hey, I'm almost there myself. Any-way, our lives aren't exactly as we planned, are they?' Sandy looked at her. 'You had a plan?'

'Well, not really, and it's just that I wonder what the future holds for us. Whether Nic will still be around in a couple of years? Where will we be?'

'You worry too much. Besides, we are not leaving

the employment of Nic Thorn until he takes us overseas. He owes us that much.'

'Good point. Shall we try Linked-In or Facebook
searches for Alexandra Ripley?'

'We could also google the West End School Yearbooks to see if there was an Alexandra in one of my
classes.'

They located some photos but found no trace
of an Alexandra in the first two. The last yearbook
referenced 'absent students', there was an Alexander Heyer listed, however, there was no image insert.
Sandy leaned back in the chair. 'OK, so she was at
school with me then. Hang on, that might be a boy's
name. Let's google that name to see what comes up.'
Rose sighed. 'This is all getting very suspicious. I think
we've been working with Nic too long.'

They googled "Alexander Heyer" but there was no
reference, so they also tried Linked-In and Facebook.
They also tried an Alexandra Heyer, but still nothing.
'Not a big deal. Not everyone uses these sites anyway.
How about we google Nic Thorn?' They did, and there
was no reference for him either.

Sandy sighed. 'Let's give up. I'll take it at face value
and get some sleep.'

They ate the lasagne, polished off a bottle of
Chardonnay, and decided to take an early night. Dog
jumped onto the couch and did a few circles before
curling up, and Rose swore the cat was smiling as she
looked back.

In the morning, Rose called Nic. 'Rise and shine, you sleepy lounge lizard. What are we up to today? I'm free, as Sandy is hooking up with Carly again.'

'Well, I have to go down to the Gold Coast to drop something off and pick up something. Are you up for that?'

'Sure, did you want to come and collect me?'

'Thought you'd never ask.'

There was a toot outside, and Sandy called out. 'Nic's here.'

'Damn you, Nic.'

Rose went outside, and Nic was in a brand-new model Tesla SUV. 'How did you know I had nothing else to do? And what's with this car? It's still a plug-in, but it looks like a slight upgrade from a Prius.'

'Boy, you ask a lot of questions. Anyway, climb in, and I'll explain it to you.... I'm delivering it to a client down the coast, but coming back might be a little up in the air.' Rose opened the door, stepped in, and punched him in the arm.

'Yow. That's my sore arm.' Rose nodded. 'Oh, poor man. Would you like me to kiss it better?'

'Sure.' Rose held his face in her hands. 'Pucker up, big boy.' Then, as he leaned forward, she punched him in the bicep of his other arm.

Nic rubbed both arms. 'You are mean this morning, aren't you? Did Dog eat your breakfast or something?'

Rose shook her head. 'Nope, just getting one back on you for the thing you made us do in Rockhampton.

You know we only work with million-dollar cars, not motorbikes.'

They took off, drove down Vulture Street, then onto the Highway heading south to the Gold Coast. Rose was desperate to avoid asking Nic about the Federal Police discharge but wanted to know more about him. 'Tell me something more about yourself. Like growing up around Ouyen and Mildura or being at school and Uni up here in Brisbane, and about that lovely twin sister called....?'

'Good try, Rose. I'm not letting that cat out of the bag. Ok, here is something then.... The Biker guy Maxie and I were both in Afghanistan in 2012. He was an Officer with UK Special Services, and I was sort of working there too, for A.S.I.O.'

'What as a tea server or a camel herder? Am I getting warmer?'

'I can't tell you otherwise I would have to kill you, and you know I don't like paperwork. I did get hammered once in a bar in Kabul, though.'

'I don't believe you. You can't drink alcohol there. It's against their custom.'

'No, actually, I was hammered with a real hammer. I was in a bar in Kabul sipping on a chai tea, and a camel was sweet on me. The owner didn't like it and ambushed me on the way out. I spent a few days in one of their lovely little stone huts until Maxie and his team rescued me.'

'You were lucky they didn't kill you.'

Nic shrugged. 'Maxie saw a lot of other things he'll never forget, though. It cost him his marriage, house, and whatever normality he expected. So, now he leads the Veteran's Bikers Club, living the dream, and helps out others occasionally. I helped him come to Australia because he couldn't face returning to the U.K.'

Rose looked over. 'Hey, slow down; I think you might be speeding. The little wheels would've fallen off if I was going this fast in a Prius, and take your hands off the wheel for a moment as your knuckles have gone white.'

Nic looked at his speed, and it was nearing 110 k.p.h. 'Oops,' and he immediately took his foot off the accelerator. The car slowed down, but there wasn't any change in the sound so Nic muttered: 'Vroom, vroom.'

Rose looked over. 'Remind me not to talk about your past when you're driving as there might be a few more memories in that old brain box you don't care to remember.' Nic continued: 'It did get me back home early. I was there about six months.'

Rose nodded. 'Even that was too long for some.'

'Yep, so now you know a little bit more about me, you'll have to forget all about it. Hey, look at that we're almost there.' Nic took the Helensvale exit and pulled the car to a stop at the train station. A well-dressed man had been waiting for them to arrive and he approached the car. 'You're two minutes late, son, which makes me five minutes late. That'll cost you an extra two thousand dollars.' Rose stepped out of the car and was about to say something, but Nic shook his head. 'Sorry, Sir. It won't happen again. I'll get the next car to you exactly two minutes earlier tomorrow.'

The man glared at Nic, stepped into the car, and drove off without saying anything more. Rose watched the car move away. 'Hey, are we catching the train back home?'

'Nope. I have an Uber picking us up and taking us to the Gold Coast airport.'

'Are we flying back?'

'Yep, I did say getting back was up in the air, didn't I?'

CHAPTER 17

The Uber driver took them to the airport, then down through the back roads, and they arrived at the hangars where the smaller planes were stored. Nic told the driver to stop, and they climbed out.

Rose looked around. 'Where to now? Are we meeting with the pilot?'

'Yep, I just have to go inside for a few minutes. Are you OK with that?' Rose nodded. 'Sure,' then went off for a walk but kept an eye on the door. Nic returned carrying a small bag and waved it at Rose. 'Ready?'

'Err...Nic, where's the pilot?'

'You've met him before, Rose.' Nic did a pirouette and faced Rose. 'Hello, Miss Palmer. My name is Nic Thorn, and I will be your pilot for your return to Brisbane.'

'Damn, you Nic. What did you do in there?'

'I lodged the trip and manifest, that sort of thing. You know I don't like paperwork, but it's all plain sailing now or plane flying, as the case may be. Have you been in one of these rattlers before?'

'How big is little, Nic?'

'Well, that's the bad news. It's a Cirrus SR20 and it's a small four-seater, but the good news is it's one of the only small planes with a parachute in the tail.'

'Good to know. I'm not so worried about the nuts and bolts in the plane. It's the one sitting in the pilot seat that concerns me. How much have you flown before?' Nic grinned. 'I have to keep my flying hours up, so I fly as often as possible. Just the bare minimum, though. It's so expensive to fly.'

Rose sighed. 'And so is crashing.'

Nic went around the little plane doing his pre-flight inspection. Checking the fuel levels, tapping on the wheels, panels and propellers, then he gave Rose the thumbs up, closed his eyes, and put his arms out as if he were blind.

Rose opened her door. 'Can we go? I'm nervous enough.'

Nic climbed into the plane, went through the pre-flight checklist, donned his headphones, and pointed to Rose to put on hers. His voice came through, and he was now all business. Rose had her eyes closed and was breathing heavily as Nic taxied to the runway.

'Tower. This is VH Delta, Delta, Tango. Seeking clearance for take-off.'

'Roger VH Delta, Delta, Tango. Cleared for take-off.'

'Here we go.' The little plane gained ground speed, Nic raised the nose, and they were airborne. 'The flight time is less than an hour. Would you like to do some sightseeing? You might have to open your eyes, though.'

'Funny, Nic. Please don't crash.'

'Nope, I've never learnt how to crash, but this plane has a great crash record. There are about six thousand made so far, but only three have ever gone down. I've heard when the parachute kicks in, it's quite a soft landing.'

'Good to know.'

Nic nodded. 'Would you like to fly it? It's just like driving a car, only that you use a yoke, and we are about five thousand metres in the air.'

'Nope, but thanks for the offer, Captain Stubing.'

Nic smiled. 'Wow, now he was a great Captain from the Love Boat TV series. You must be nervous as you just quoted pop culture to me.'

Rose finally opened her eyes. 'Yes, as that was another re-run that Father allowed my brother and I to watch. Father thought it would broaden our world. I had to explain to him it was made on a TV studio lot in LA.'

Nic grinned. 'So, how's the flight so far?'

Rose grimaced. 'Well, I've never been in a plane this small before. It is interesting, and I'm not yet comfortable with it, but at least it has opened my eyes to the experience. Why are you flying it?'

'I've just brokered the sale of this little flapper. This one is worth about four hundred grand, and I am making quite a bit on the flip. By the way, we're looking for a big brown coloured snake down below. It's called the Brisbane River.'

'OK. I think it's below us. What do we need to find next? How about the airport runway?'

Nic nodded. 'Yep, good tip. It's the flat black thing that's not the Ipswich Motorway. Landing on cars is bad; landing on the tarmac is good. Ready to take her down?' Rose nodded quickly. 'Yes, please.'

'Tower, this is VH Delta, Delta, Tango. Seeking clearance for landing on 28L.'

'Roger VH Delta, Delta, Tango. Cleared for landing.'

Nic lined up the runway, brought the plane to stalling speed, and was about to touch down when a call came through the headphones:

'All available. Full land and sea search required. Russell Island. Confirm.'

Nic pulled back on the throttle, switched the radio to another channel, and responded through his microphone.

'This is VH Delta, Delta, Tango. Confirming availability to assist.

'Estimated flight time is twenty minutes. Over.'

The plane gained height; 'Sorry, Rose, we've got to take off again. That was an emergency call for assistance. A plane has gone down near Russell Island, and we're going to assist the land and sea search.'

'So, I heard. Can't you leave me here? We're close to the ground. I could jump.'

'Sorry, no can do; the weight manifest would need to be amended, and I'd have to do the paperwork.'

'Damn you, Nic.'

Nic turned the plane in an easterly direction, and they reached cruising altitude again. 'At least this time, if we have to go down, it will be a softer landing on the water.' Rose leaned forward to put her head into her hands. 'Water still feels like cement when falling from a height; besides that, do we have enough fuel?'

'Enough to get us to Russell Island. We can always come back on the ferry.'

'Can you put the plane onto the ferry? I don't get it anyway; how can a plane be lost? Don't planes have transponders? And what about the radar? And what about using eyewitnesses? Someone must have seen something?'

'Boy, you ask a lot of questions.' Nic steadied the plane and continued: 'Well, the transponder must be turned off which makes the little blip disappear from the radar. Pilots can turn them off if safety is an issue, or to avoid radar detection, of course, they must've read that chapter in the instruction manual.'

'Why would anyone do that?'

'Read the manual? It's always a good idea to read the instructions. I guess it can't have been a male pilot if that's the case.'

'Nope, you dope. Turn off the radar.'

'A couple of reasons. One I can think of straight away... to steal a plane.'

'Is everything about fraud and scams with you?'
Nic shook his head. 'Not everything, but most things.
It's where my mind goes whenever there is something
fishy, and speaking of big fishy, keep a lookout and as
we might see some whales.'

Rose took a deep breath and decided to look out
of the window. 'I haven't seen the Brisbane islands
from up here before. They're quite pretty, aren't they?
There are seven main ones and lots of little ones that
you can take a day trip to for a romantic interlude.'
Nic grinned. 'Speaking from experience?'

'Some. That's something I can do, operate a run-a-
bout. I once left a guy on Peel Island, it's the one clos-
est to Cleveland Point. He was getting a bit handsy, so
I told him to go for a swim to cool off, then I took the
boat across to North Stradbroke to get away, and rode
the ferry home.'

'Is he still there?'

'I'm not sure, it was about five years ago and I
haven't been back to check.'

'Wow, remind me never to take you on a date to
a remote island.' Rose looked over. 'Are we ever going
on a date?' Nic shrugged and then leaned forward to
change the radio volume to get an update on the
search.

'This is VH Delta, Delta, Tango.
Just flying over to Long Island. Over.'
'Roger, VH Delta, Delta, Tango. This is Marine
Rescue. Head west.

Two other planes in the air. Switch to channel 71.'

Nic tuned the radio, and they could listen to the banter from everyone involved in the search party, however, there wasn't much talk. Rose looked out the window to Russell Island in the foreground. 'Is there a runway on the island?'

'Nope.'

'So, you heard that question, but not the one about going on a date?'

'I wasn't ignoring you. I thought we were on a date. You must admit that flying in a plane is much better than being in a balloon. I can't get handsy as I have to keep my hands on the wheel.' Rose nodded. 'You could use autopilot.'

'Damn, why didn't I think of that?'

Rose looked over. 'Always keep your hands on the wheel and body parts inside the plane.' Nic then did a low sweep in the plane and tuned back into the radio:

'This is VH Delta, Delta, Tango. Nothing to report. Over.'

'Please bear north. Over.

Roger that. Over.'

Nic turned the radio down and tapped at his microphone. 'Is there anything else you'd like to look at whilst we have this wonderful sightseeing opportunity?'

Rose leaned a little forward. 'Well, can we see where those dodgy land allotments were set up on Russell Island? What a scam that was. Well before my time, it was in the early seventies. I think about fourteen thousand land lots were sold at the last count.'

Nic nodded. 'Sure, can do. I studied that case as part of my thesis on land scams and major property frauds. I was part of a team that made a formal report to the Ministerial Enquiry into it. Oops, ignore that statement. I read about it in the back of a door once. It was a big door.'

Rose looked over to Nic. 'Is that right? So, tell me more about this study you did, and would you like Sandy and me to study something so we can be better educated about handling all of this stuff we do with you?'

'Nope and nope. Nope to the first one, and nope to the second, just in case you misunderstood me.'

CHAPTER 18

Nic headed north, and they were now flying over Russell Island. 'See the land below us…back in the day, a developer found a nice government ear to sponsor him into subdividing the land for future use. It was re-zoned residential, and then the fun began. They were selling them as underdeveloped sites without power, water, or sewage. No services would be connected as part of the sale, and at one stage, they talked about building a bridge between the mainland and the island.' Rose nodded. 'So, I'd read.'

Nic continued. 'Then the tide came in and swallowed up the land. They'd sold some of the sites at low tide. People were furious, and even years later, as in almost fifty years, there are still landowners down there who haven't been able to sell. The local government has been doing a buy-back ever since.'

Rose shook her head. 'And yet the developer got away with it?'

'Something like that, but the finding also showed the council was complicit in the sales and development. There are about eight hundred blocks around the island, and it's getting even murkier now, as it turns out the council didn't have the power to stop the development of any of the sites, not just the ones underwater. Some of them are selling now for around two hundred thousand.'

Nic nodded towards a large machinery shed underneath them. It appeared to have direct water access and was well away from any prying eyes. 'I think we should get someone to look at that.' He turned up the radio on Channel 71.

'This is VH Delta, Delta, Tango, currently over Melomy's Wetland.

Does anyone know of a large shed being built down there? Over.'

'This is Marine Rescue. We haven't been in the area. Over.'

Nic nodded. 'Well, Rose, it looks like we're going to be landing sooner than I expected.' Rose looked out the window. 'I didn't think there was an airport.'

'There isn't. We're doing a sea landing. This beauty has been modified with floats. You'll need to crank the handles in the back, and the wheels go up.'

Rose turned her head and saw the handles on each side of the inner sides of the plane. 'I guess you want me to climb back there then?'

'Well, you said you didn't want to fly the plane.'

Rose unclipped her seatbelt and maneuvered herself through the gap between the chairs. 'Is this as simple as it looks? It reads 'unclip the handle – turn twice 360°."

'Yep, it's on a ratio pulley system. Just let it do the work.'

Rose followed the instructions, and Nic leaned out his window to check the floats were in place. 'Good job. Now the fun begins; we're going down.'

Nic tuned into the radio:

This is VH Delta, Delta, Tango.
We're heading down for a water landing. Over.
Roger that.

The little plane skipped quietly over the water and bumped slowly onto the sandy beach just a little south of where Nic had seen the large shed. 'How was that for a great water landing?'

Rose shrugged. 'Either way, you look at it, I won't be flying back with you. I'll call an Uber and take the ferry back.'

'OK with me, but check your phone. Do you have any service?'

Rose extracted the phone and held it up, looking for a signal. 'Damn, you Nic.'

Nic climbed out and secured the plane to the nearest tree with a rope. 'I reckon we've got about a ten-minute walk to the site. Hopefully, there's no one there. If there is, we'll have to explain we're running short on fuel and had to land.'

'Are we running short on fuel, and did we have to land?'

Nic shook his head. 'I guess we'll find out when we take off.' Nic then leaned into the plane's rear and removed a small barrel bag from beneath the back seat. 'I've got a change of clothes in here, so before we head off, let's get out of these civvies and into something more...um, like walkies.'

Rose stepped out of the plane. 'Did you bring something for me too?'

'Of course.'

'Of course, what? How did you know I would need a change of clothes?'

'Well, ever since the last time I made you pirouette through the waterfall at GOMA and go home all soggy in the back of a taxi, I thought it would be a good idea.' Nic held up a stylish trekking tracksuit for her. It was Rose's size. 'I think these will fit; Sandy helped me pick them out.'

'Do you have any shoes for me?'

'Yep.' Nic held up a pair of hiking boots. 'These should work.'

Rose stepped around to the other side of the plane and changed into the new outfit, whilst Nic stayed where he was. 'Are you ready to go wandering? My Batman senses tell me the lost plane will likely be found inside the shed.' Rose tied her shoelaces, stood up, and stretched. 'What if we do find something? How are we going to phone it in?'

Nic pulled out his phone and shook it lightly. 'I

have service. Remind me to provide you with a satellite phone next time we have to go hiking.'

Rose sighed. 'We're only a short ferry ride from the mainland and yet, I don't have any service.' Nic nodded. Well, blame the telco's, not me.'

The walk took around fifteen minutes through the scrub, and finally, Nic held up his hand to let Rose know they were to stop. He crouched down and indicated for her to do as well. 'I can't hear anything, so wait here, and I'll get closer.' Nic handed over the phone, and Rose grinned. 'Would you like me to call for backup or an Uber?'

'Radio silence at the moment. I'll be back in a jiff.'

Rose watched Nic clamber through the scrub and he lay prostrate on the brush as he got nearer, then pulled a small monocular from his pocket. Nic appeared satisfied that the place was vacant as he stood up. However, Rose thought she saw movement at one of the windows, cupped her hands in front of her mouth and let out an almighty call. 'Brackagh, brackagh.'

Nic must've heard or seen something, too, as he slowly lowered himself down again, then scrambled back to Rose. 'Did you hear that? It sounded like the mating call of an extinct duck called the Thorn Bud Warbler. They're quite rare, you know.'

Rose shrugged. 'It was me. I thought I saw something at the window. I think there's someone in there.'

'Nope. I would say there's been no one here for

hours. There's an alarm dial on the front door, and it looks like it was turned on about three hours ago.'

'That's not good then, is it?'

'Actually, it is good as it means there might be something valuable there.'

They headed for the shed, and Rose searched the roof joists for cameras in case they were being filmed. Nic nodded upwards. 'There are no cameras yet if that's what you're looking for as there is an unopened box on the front stoop marked: "Security Cameras – to be installed by a licensed electrician only."

Rose shook her head. 'Wow, why would that stop someone? They steal a plane, but don't open a box marked with a warning.'

'I know Rose, people are bad.'

Nic went towards the front door and used his phone to take a photograph of the lock, then sent it to Chewy. They waited for the response. 'This lock looks new. Chewy should be able to find the specs on the net and whether it has any security deficiencies.'

The lock chimed, and the display read. 'Open.'

Nic's phone then buzzed with a message:

New lock. Still at factory setting – 0000.

Linked to a satellite com network.

As it was early afternoon, sufficient light was coming into the building for them to look around. Nic pulled another gizmo from another pocket, turned it on and waved it into the space, and it immediately started beeping. 'This is the latest tool in my arsenal of finding stuff. It sends out a radar beam and picks up different types of metals. I've currently got it set on 'find a plane.' Nic moved forward into the large shed and pointed towards the rear. 'That's what we are looking for. I'll go down there, and you stay up this end.' There was a Seaplane parked in the rear of the shed. 'Don't you love when a plan comes together?'

Nic opened the door of the Sea Plane, turned the transponder on to check it was working, and then called Marine Rescue on his satellite phone: 'I've found the plane. The transponder was turned off.'

'Roger and Out.'

Rose started moving around the shed and noticed several metal cases - whilst closed, none were pad-locked. Rose pulled down on the sleeve of her wind-cheater to cover her fingertips whilst she lifted the lid and peered inside. It was full of designer handbags. 'Nic, I think we're onto something here.' Rose opened another case containing various jewellery pieces. Some were still in the original boxes, unopened. An-other box had designer shoes; some were still in their original boxes. 'These shoes are genuine. I'd recognise a fake if I saw one. There are thousands of dollars of stuff in here.'

Nic called out from further down the garage. 'Make that tens of thousands. There's five brand new Sea-Doo's down here and a Haines Hunter runabout. This Sea Wind aeroplane is about twenty years old, but still worth around two hundred thousand. Someone has been very busy.'

'Do we call the Fraud Squad?'

'They would most likely have to come from the mainland. Besides, we don't know what this is. It might all be legit. Let's keep looking.'

Rose called back. 'Apart from a plane that could've been stolen.'

'There is that.' Nic was walking towards Rose when he passed what appeared to be a row of large boards covered by a tarpaulin. He called Rose over, and they removed the canvas sheet. Three whiteboards were covered in diagrams, circles, and lines. In the middle was a set of names, places, and dates. On the left-hand side panel, there was a small photograph of a smiling, well-dressed man.

Nic tapped the picture. 'That's Bernie Madoff.'

Rose nodded. 'Ponzi fraudster in the extreme, he got away with fifty million until his family dobbed him in. Last I heard, he was serving one hundred and fifty years in jail. Just what have we stumbled into here?'

Nic smiled. 'I would say this is ground zero of whatever this is. Whoever is behind all of this is using this remote site to coordinate their operations. It's very comprehensive, so let's keep looking to see if we can find a name or something.'

CHAPTER 19

Rose continued looking through the space when she noticed a three-door filing cabinet. This time, as it was locked, she called Nic over to look. 'Should we look to see what's inside? It's the only thing in here that's locked. Maybe it means something.'

Nic pulled from his jacket pocket a little black case, unzipped it and held it open for Rose to see. 'More tools of the trade. These little things are the keys to solving lots of mysteries.'

'They look like keys to break into things.'

'That too, but I don't break anything. I'm cautious about that. Generally, they're left in the same condition I found them.'

'Isn't it a little illegal?'

Nic pulled a couple of slender picks from the case and pushed them slowly into the lock. 'Could be...but it depends on...whoops, the cabinet was already unlocked. We should've checked that first.'

'I did.'

Nic grinned. 'Oh, you must've had a man look, as it's unlocked now.'

Rose shook her head, then moved away to look for other crates.

Nic slid the top drawer out. There were various files; the first folder was the thickest, containing newspaper clippings and internet printouts about Bernie Madoff worldwide. He flicked through and saw the most recent addition was Madoff's parole attempt in June 2020. It had been unsuccessful. Others had a named label and contained various printouts, photographs, and notes.

Flicking through them quickly, he stopped when he saw the name, Alexandra Ripley. Nic raised the folder and peered inside. It contained an Australian Passport, so he carefully lifted it, opened it to the portrait, and recognised it as the same woman perpetrating the fraudulent loan under Sandy's name. It was also the same woman who had leapt from the stage at the fraud presentation in Brisbane some months earlier. He took a photograph, returned the passport and slid the file into place.

There was another large folder near the back, so he pulled that one up. It read: Lucas Wilts – U.S. Ambassador.' A yellow post-it note was attached to the first page: 'Cha Cha Grill Monday 19th 7 p.m.' Nic removed the note, placed it flat on the top of the draw and photographed it and knew whatever plans he had for tonight would have to change.

Nic then placed it back, filed through the remainder of the folders, and saw the name: 'Sandra Fraser.'

He extracted the file. It also contained a passport; again, it was a portrait of the same woman. Nic closed the drawer and re-locked the cabinet. 'Rose, I think it's time we leave here.'

They re-shrouded the whiteboards, and Nic took pictures of the surroundings with his phone. They re-traced their steps and were back outside in the sunshine.

'Ready to go home now?'

They headed towards the plane, and Nic added: 'I still have to deliver it back to Archerfield airport.'

'Damn you, Nic.'

'It's only about thirty minutes or so.'

'How will you explain why we are five hours late?'

'I'll make something up. I could say I have engine trouble, but that wouldn't go down too well.'

The flight back took about forty minutes as Nic had taken a scenic flight over Brisbane and Mt. Coo-tha. Rose had undoubtedly had enough when they finally landed.

Nic turned the engine off and removed his head-set. 'What a nice day. We drove a nice car, flew in a nice plane, and discovered a not-so-nice, alleged fraudster's secret lair. Does it count as a first date? What was your highlight?'

Rose smiled. 'Finally landing at Archerfield.'

Nic shook his head. 'At least I tried to keep you entertained. Anyway, can you keep the Russell Island thing on the down low, even from Sandy? We don't know what we're up against, and it might get ugly.'

Rose was about to disembark when she remembered to collect the bag of clothing. 'If the plane's transponder was working, why would the pilot turn it off if the plane wasn't stolen?'

Nic smiled. 'Most likely, if the pilot had already turned off the radar to avoid detection, they would've wanted to hide the plane too. Turn the transponder off, and the plane disappears. Clever, but not clever enough for Nic Thorn and Associates.'

They met with the new owner, completed the paperwork and Sandy was waiting for them in the car-park. 'How was the flight, Rose?'

'It had its ups and downs. How did your meeting with Alexandra go?'

'Let's get in the car, and I'll tell you all about it.'

They went to the car, and it was neighbour Dave's Hyundai. 'I've had to borrow it from Dave as you haven't yet returned the Peugeot. Our little S-Cargo doesn't seat three people.'

Nic called out. 'Hey, I'm working on getting the car back. By the way, it's my shout for dinner as that plane deal just made me about forty grand.'

Rose looked at him. 'Why do we need to know that?'

'Well, you told me you'd like to know how I get money to fund your lavish lifestyles.'

'OK. What's for dinner then? What's around here

anyway? Where can we celebrate at KFC or Hungry Jacks?'

'Nope, they're too high-brow for me. Let's lash out, drop me home, and meet at Cha Cha Cha Grill around seven. I know you guys like upmarket, high-quality food, and I take all my best workers there. I never let them order anything, just let them stare through the window and read the menu at the front door.'

Rose nodded. 'It's a real first date then, Nic?'

'No, Rose. It's a job.'

They dropped Nic at his South Bank apartment, then went home to West End, fed Dog, checked on Dave, and thanked him for the use of the car.

At about 6:30 p.m., they caught the ferry around Riverside and entered the restaurant. Nic was already there waiting, and he stood to greet them. 'Thank you for coming. You both look wonderful tonight. We have so much to talk about.'

Rose sat down, leaned over, and whispered. 'Is someone in earshot that you want to impress? Why are you being so nice to us? Besides, your eye is twitching again. You're acting, aren't you?'

Nic held a finger to his eye, leaned forward and whispered back. 'There's a party behind me that I don't want to hear anything about me or us. So, we either go somewhere else or keep our conversations to a minimum.'

'Let's stay here. So, who are they?' Sandy whispered, leaning into now, too.

'I'll tell you later.' Nic then leaned back in his chair. 'Now, ladies, let's get this celebration under-way. I've been on the phone with the Victoria's Secret Modelling Agency, and we are due to complete the negotiation of your contract's later this week. Con-gratulations to both of you.' Nic leaned forward again and whispered. 'Did that get anyone's attention from behind me?'

Rose shook her head. 'I don't think so. Maybe they don't think we're VS modelling material, or they could be deaf.'

Sandy whispered, 'Or blind, but I don't see any Guide Dogs under their table.' Rose ignored the comment. 'How was the meeting with Alexandra Ripley?'

'That was weird. She didn't turn up. I rang her number, and it went straight to the message bank. She didn't return the call either. I waited for an hour.'

'Do you think it's legit then?'

'No idea. Maybe her phone battery was flattery or something. It doesn't matter; if it's important, she'll contact me again.'

'What are you guys talking about?'

Sandy continued: 'Oh, I didn't realise you weren't in the loop. On the way back from Rockhampton, I got a call from Alexandra Ripley. She said she was from West End Primary School and wanted to get together to plan a school reunion. Rose and I couldn't remem-ber the name. Mind you, I was only about six years old. Otherwise, I don't think I've ever met her.'

They stopped talking as the waiter came over to take their orders. Sandy and Rose went with the glazed eggplant for the entree, then Fish of the Day for the mains, just to annoy Nic. He ordered Oysters Kilpatrick, then the Wagyu Rump.

Rose leaned over to Nic. 'We aren't meat eaters. You might have noticed by now.' Nic called the waiter back and changed his mains to the Cha Cha Cha Sausages. 'There's still meat in sausages, Nic.'

'I'll pick the meat out. Besides, I wanted to try the colcannon that it's served with. It sounds so exotic.'

'That's just a posh way of serving mashed potato with cabbage.'

'All good then. So, what happened to this mystery girlfriend hook-up? Did you find out anything more?'

'Nope, but Rose and I googled the school yearbooks. We could only find a record of an Alexander, not an Alexandra. No photo, and he was absent on the day of the shoot. Nothing on Facebook or LinkedIn either.'

'Do you want me to get Chewy to check it out? He loves a good Scooby Doo mystery.'

Sandy shook her head. 'Not yet, thanks, but surely this is too trivial for the likes of the services of Nic Thorn and Associates, but thanks for the offer.'

The meal came, they ate, and Nic quietly filled them on the latest developments with the cattle duffing. 'All the cows are fine, but no one can talk cow to check with them anyway.' Nic then got up to leave. 'That group are still behind me, aren't they?'

'Yes, so will you tell us who they are then?'

'Nup. Are you free tomorrow to deliver another car down to the coast?'

'Yep, are we flying again? I've seen all of Brisbane I need to see from the air.'

'No, whatever floats your boat, Rose. See you at the same time again tomorrow then.' He went off, settled the bill, deliberately avoided looking back at them, and exited.

Rose looked at Sandy. 'I think we should take a picture of us celebrating the Victoria's Secret Modelling contracts. Have you got your phone handy?'

'We didn't get the contracts, Rose.'

'I know that, but I'm just interested in knowing why Nic avoided this group behind us. Ask them to take a selfie of us with all of them in the background. Set it on panoramic.' Sandy went over to the group, introduced herself, pointed to Rose, and handed one of the women her phone. Rose and Sandy posed and took a selfie with the group featuring behind them. Sandy checked the picture. It had caught most of the group, and the woman sat back down. 'I'm so sorry. I had the set-up around the wrong way. Would you mind retaking it, please? We're celebrating our appointments as Victoria's Secret models in New York.'

This time, one of the men stood up. 'Well, ladies, it's your lucky day.' He had a hint of an American accent, and Rose glanced over to Sandy as he continued. 'I know the guys at L Brands. I overheard ya Agent say that you'd just won the contracts. It'll be great to see some more of ya Aussies since Miranda has given it away and gone over to I.M.G.'

Sandy went blank, but Rose piped up. 'Sorry, our manager made all the arrangements for us. We're not sure.'

'Let me take your photo anyway.'

'Sorry, sir, again we're not sure. Just leave me your details, and I'll check that out with our management.' He nodded, took their photo, and handed over his business card: Lucas Wilts, Australian Consul-General,

New York, 150 E 42nd, New York, NY 1001. United States.'

'Thank you anyway, ladies. When you get over there, ya 'all have your photos taken by everybody, so good luck, and ya 'all look me up. I'd love to show some VS models around the Big Apple.'

Rose and Sandy quickly nodded and moved away. They collected the rest of their belongings, went out to Eagle Street and took a taxi home.

When they finally sat down, Sandy let out her breath. 'Whoa, that was close. We aren't so good at this secret squirrel stuff, are we? You bounced in pretty quickly. I had no idea what to do.'

'Yes, but now we have the picture of the group, what do we do? We only know Nic's people do this sort of thing. We don't have people like his people.'

Sandy nodded. 'And on that note, I'm going to bed. This world of spies, waterfalls, fights, cattle duffing, dodgy invoicing, and marriage scams suddenly makes me very tired.'

'Don't forget all the fishy stuff we do, but for one brief moment, we were taken seriously as Victoria's Secret Models. Is that the future for us? Can we do that sort of thing?'

'Seriously, Rose?'

'No, who would look after Nic, and help him spend his money?'

In the meantime, Nic had been waiting patiently outside the restaurant and he watched Rose and Sandy leave. He wanted to meet with Lucas Wilts. The man eventually came out to have a cigarette and was leaning against the boardwalk's balustrade, staring at the river.

Nic moved up to him. 'Nice night.'

'Y'all right there, my man.'

'You're an American?'

The man nodded. 'No. I've been living in New York and picked up a bit of the local twang.' Nic thought about the best way to broach the subject of Alexandra Ripley. 'I've heard the life of an Ambassador is lonely.'

The man looked at him. 'I didn't tell you what I did.'

'That you didn't, but the two women you took the photo with are my associates, and I wanted to know who you were and what you wanted with them. I saw you talking to them.' Nic hoped that the ploy would work, despite having already left the restaurant.

The man took a pull on his cigarette and blew the smoke from the corner of his mouth. 'They said they were VS models.' He said no more and took another draw on the cigarette.

Nic didn't know whether that meant he suspected they weren't or that he did, so he decided to get straight to the point. 'Do you know an Alexandra Ripley?'

Wilts looked at him. 'Who is she?'

'How about Bernie Madoff?'

'Of course, I know who he is. What has Alex got to do with Bernie Madoff? I'm meeting her tomorrow night at Alchemy Restaurant for late drinks.'

'Good. I was checking that she wasn't at your party in there. Just be careful.'

Nic mock saluted and moved away, then made a phone call: 'She wasn't there, but he's meeting her at Alchemy tomorrow night. My eyes only.'

CHAPTER 20

At 9 a.m. the following morning, Nic was waiting outside Sandy's place and had arrived in a red Tesla Model X. The gull-wing doors were open, and he was standing next to it watching Rose trying to prevent Dog from harassing a wounded sparrow. The bird appeared to feign the injury, and Dog didn't look impressed.

Nic leaned into the car and tooted the horn. 'Morning Rose, I must get down to the coast. It is such a chore having to drive these boring little cars. This one's about a hundred and fifty grand worth and doesn't have the toe warmers. It has the heated seats and warmed seatbelts, but they skimped on keeping your little toes warm.' The bird flew away, and Dog sauntered off.

'You're an idiot, Nic.'

'I know, but at least your mother likes me. I'm glad you've dressed warmly, as there's a chance we could get wet on the way back.'

'Damn, you Nic. Are we off to Helensvale Railway Station to meet with 'Mr Grumpy Pants' again?'

'Nope. We are going direct to Sanctuary Cove to drop this little beauty off. I'm still meeting up with Mr Grumpy Pants, though. By the way, where's Sandy?'

'She's not coming; Alexandra rang again this morning and wants to meet at 4 p.m. at The Coffee Club in Brisbane Square. Will we be back by then?'

'Yep. Are you good to go? Jump in my rosy, risky rascal and off to the cat cave.'

'What cat cave?'

'Catamarans Rose, 'The Sanctuary Cove Boat Show' is where we're headed. I hope you don't get seasick as we return to Brisbane in a speedboat.'

'OK, as long as we don't get airborne again. I should be fine.'

'Sorry, I can't promise you that. We might not be flying in the air, but the boat does have a top speed of fifty knots.'

Sandy came out to wave them goodbye, and Dog sniffed the air, then meowed loudly. 'Cripes. I thought you would have fed the cat already.'

'We have. It's just his way of saying I'm awake, so look out, world.'

'Duly noted. I'm like that too if I haven't had my morning chai tea by nine o'clock.'

Nic remotely opened the doors, climbed in and drove off. 'It's about fifty minutes to get down there. We have to be two minutes early, too, so Mister Grumpy Pants doesn't dock me the two grand again. What do you want to ask me about today, Rose?'

They moved out on the freeway, and Nic set the cruise control on the car to 110 k.p.h., momentarily took both hands off the wheel and crossed his arms. Rose tapped at his arm. 'You can't do that, you dope; you're not driving an X-Box.'

'Oops, sorry, I thought everything was remote control in this car. It should be, as they're just so damn expensive.' He put his hands back on the wheel and Rose continued: 'OK. My question today....mm. Why did you want to avoid the Australian Consul-General, based in New York, at last night's dinner? And who were the rest of them?'

'Wow, how did you work that out?'

'Well, once he knew we were both Victoria's Secret Models, he told us all his secrets. It's just what beautiful people have to contend with sometimes.'

'I guess so. Anyway, I'm going to tell you something else about me now. The more you know, the more you might not want to know. You know?'

'No, I think I'm adult enough to handle stuff. I know stuff about my Father's stuff, and he keeps telling me more stuff, too. One day, all the stuffing in my head might fall out and that's what I'm afraid of.'

'I've taught you well. You talk gobble-de-gook, and I seem to understand.'

Rose shrugged. 'So, what's your stuff all about then?'

Nic hesitated. 'I was.... I used to work for the Australian Security Intelligence Organisation. I was based in Canberra and had a few postings overseas. I went to New York a couple of times, Washington too.'

Nic took a breath and continued. 'Anyway, once in March 2014, I met and dined with Obama and Mrs Obama. She said I was a good-looking young man. I thought that was weird.'

'Well, you probably were a good-looking man back then. He is not as good-looking as Benoit Trudeau, but no one is as good-looking as him, not even Brad Pitt. Why was it weird?'

'Well, with all that was going on in the Obama's world, the Presidency, that sort of stuff, she noticed how good-looking I was. It made me feel like eye candy, and coming from the First Lady, I didn't know how to take it.'

'So, what did you say back to her?'

'The best I could do was thank her, but then I said, 'and so is your husband', and that's when she whispered to me if I thought he was the best-looking President ever. I thought that was a bit weird.'

'Why was that weird?'

'The First Lady of the United States just winked at me.'

Nic pulled the Tesla into the carpark at Sanctuary Cove, and Mr Grumpy Pants was again waiting for them. He came up, and Nic lowered the window. 'You're two minutes early this time. I'll have to give the two thousand dollars back now.'

Nic lowered his head. 'Sorry, sir, but I can drive around the block for you.'

The elderly man waggled his index finger at Nic, then went around to help Rose climb out. 'And don't get smart with me, young man. You're not so old that I can't put you over my knee.' Nic exited the car, and the man drove off without another word. 'He's nasty, Nic, how much business do you do with him?'

'Not much, but he is my uncle. It's hard to do business with family. I think you know that all too well, don't you.'

'Damn, you Nic.'

Nic laughed. 'And don't bother to ask him about my sister, as he doesn't know her name either.'

They went off to get an early lunch and down to the quay. Nic looked around at all the food stalls. 'It might not be a good idea to have a big lunch; otherwise, the trip back may get messy for both of us.'

They decided on a couple of sliders. Rose chose the vegetarian option and ambled along the esplanade, looking at the boats. 'So, which one are we taking back? Big enough for two captains and ten crew?'

'Nope, we've just got a two-seater. It's not very big, but very fast.'

Rose watched as a very sleek black boat came towards them. The bow was riding high, the two engines growling louder than Nic's Mustang. The skipper pulled it to a stop. He looked about seventy years old and had a big grin. The man stayed in the and beckoned Nic to join him.

'Yes, thank you, Mr Thorn, I'll buy it. My wife is going to love it. The boys back home will not believe my new fishing boat is a Brabus Shadow 500 T-top. I'll drive to Brisbane, pick up my wife and then we'll meet you at Raby Bay Quay. Make sure it's ready.'

Nic assisted Rose to board. 'This is what we're going back to Brisbane in, and be careful getting in. It's about six hundred thousand dollars worth.'

'Lucky I'm wearing my soft boat shoes then.'

'PFDs are stored in the front. Please grab one for me, too.' Nic then shook the man's hand and assisted him to alight. 'I told you, didn't I? This craft is about the best fun you can have on the water.'

Rose whispered. 'That sounded a bit contrived.'

Nic smiled and then whispered to Rose. 'Well, I've been chasing this deal down for months. It's a combined wedding and birthday present he's giving his new wife. I had to convince him not to paint it pink, but we still had to dress it up with a big ribbon and flowers when we arrived back at Raby Bay.'

'Nice to know I have my uses and good to see love conquers all. Even for the oldies.' Nic nodded a final goodbye to the buyer, and they pushed off.

A small crowd had gathered to see what was making all the noise, so he pushed the throttle, and the engines roared to life, much to the cheer of the gathered group and it wasn't long before the boat was in its element in the open water. Nic managed to keep it under control, but the water chop meant it was bucking like a bronco. They dropped into a wave trough, bounced out, and Nic called over the din. 'We've only had about twenty minutes to go.'

They passed Cassim Island off the Redland Bay coastline, rounded the point alongside the Lighthouse Restaurant, and Nic throttled back. 'See, we made it safe and sound, but that's the last time I try to tame one of these beasts. I'm delivering it to the quay at Raby Bay, that's when we add the ribbons and bows.'

'So, there's still time for me to grab the train and meet Sandy at the Coffee Club in the city. Did you want to come too?'

'Nup, I've got some stuff to do here. You go, and I'll catch up with you later. Are you doing anything tomorrow?'

'No, why?'

'Well, it looks like you cope with planes and boats. How are you with rockets and floating in zero gravity?'

Rose looked at him horrified. 'You are kidding, aren't you?'

Nic smiled and slowed the boat to trawling speed to enter the quay.

Two guys dressed in 'Raby Bay Harbour' shirts threw ropes and cleated them off. Nic stopped the engine. 'Thanks, guys. This Brabus is the real deal. Did you bring along the ribbon and flowers?'

They nodded to a couple of cardboard boxes next

to them on the dock; then, Nic helped Rose climb out of the boat. Fifteen minutes later, Rose and Nic had tied a sizeable pink ribbon across the bow and opened the boxes of flowers. They were pink Lisianthus, at least five bouquets containing ten flowers each. The elderly man they'd met at Sanctuary Cove was arm in arm with a woman, and she appeared to be about twenty-five years old. Another woman trailed behind them, pushing a pram containing two Labrador puppies.

Rose looked at them and then at Nic. 'Ah, ain't young love grand.'

The young woman de-linked arms with her beau and rushed toward the boat. 'Daddy, what have you bought for me? It's beautiful.'

Rose stepped away but not before whispering: 'I thought you said she was his new wife; she just called him Daddy.'

'Yep, she did. They met on the dating site, 'Sugar Daddies Looking for Love.''

Rose sighed. 'Damn, I used that other dating app, Vita Brevis, and only found you. I could've had a speed boat instead.'

Nic smiled, and Rose began to walk away. 'Anyway, I'm off, so I'll catch you tomorrow. What've you got lined up for me to do next?'

'Nothing, take the day off.'

Rose walked over to the train station, caught the Express Train into Brisbane City, and walked down

Ann Street to the Brisbane City Town Hall Coffee Club. Sandy was already there and sat down. 'Hey, you made it then?'

'Yes, it was a rough boat ride up the bay. Have you ordered?'

'Nope. I'm still waiting for Alexandra. It's just four now. She's due any minute.'

Rose continued: 'Anyway, Nic said the boat was worth about six hundred thousand. The elderly gentleman bought it for his twenty-five-year-old wife as a joint wedding and birthday present. He was forty-five years older than her, so it looks like I used the wrong dating site a year ago. I only found Nic, as all he has given us is trouble.' They laughed, ordered coffee and cake, and sat there waiting.

It was 4.30 p.m. when Sandy's phone rang. 'Hi, Alexandra..... OK, sorry, I didn't realise. Rose is my best friend. OK, let's do it another time.' Sandy put the phone down on the table. 'I think I just got told off. She wanted to know why I wasn't alone and why I had disobeyed her instructions.'

'You're right; it's getting bizarre. Is she going to meet up with you again?'

'Yes. We're meeting again at another Coffee Club on Wednesday; this time, it's at the one down at Sherwood. I don't know why we can't return to the same one. Oh, I was informed you can't come.'

Rose nodded. 'OK. Let's go home.'

CHAPTER 21

It was another warm night in Brisbane, and Sandy, Rose, Dave, and Dog were sitting out on the back deck. 'Hey, Dave. I asked Nic about the Federal Police discharge thing. He said he was with the Australian Security Intelligence Organisation, not the AFP.'

'OK, Albert might have got that wrong. Wow, A.S.I.O., that is big-time spy stuff.'

Sandy interjected. 'What are you guys talking about?'

'Dave took a phone call from Uncle Albert when he was in the hospital and tried to tell him it wasn't you, but he kept talking anyway. He'd said he'd completed a Probity check on Nic. He was dishonourably discharged from the AFP, but Nic told me today that he worked with A.S.I.O.'

'Albert did tell me once about a guy he knew who was a spy. I just thought he was raving. He muttered something about having to kill himself as he had given up the secret to me. Of course, I didn't think he was serious.'

Dave nodded. 'Now that we all know, does it make any difference to how you feel about Nic?'

Rose shook her head. 'Not really. It makes me feel even better about him. It does explain how he manages to link up with all these scams he gets us into. He must have many contacts in a lot of Government Departments. We should stop calling him Batman because he's a spy. Maybe use 'Bond, Nic Bond.'''

Dave nodded. 'Maybe Thorn is not even his real name. We should google 'Nic Bond' to see what turns up.'

Rose grabbed her phone and keyed in the name to the browser, but it returned with a fetish reference to stealing underwear from clotheslines; "*Knicker Nickers*". They laughed, and then Dog suddenly stopped licking his food bowl and looked towards the backyard.

Dave noticed. 'Dog's stopped eating, guys, something must be up.'

'Yep, he's our watch cat. The last time he did that was when Rose's ex-husband was visiting.'

A female voice called out from the darkness. 'Hello, Sandy. Are you there?'

'On the back deck. Who is it?'

'Alexandra Ripley.'

The women looked at each other. 'How did she know where I lived?'

The woman came to the bottom of the deck stairs and looked up. 'Is that Rose there with you too?' She then started ascending the stairs, but just as she got to the decking platform, Dog hissed at her and took off inside.

Dave stood up. 'That's my cue to go then, guys. I'll leave you to it. Thanks for dinner, guys.' He nodded at them and headed down the stairs to go home. Alexandra watched him leave. 'I'm glad I finally found you at home. I thought we'd not bother with another attempt at The Coffee Club, so I came here instead. Hope that's OK.'

'Not really, Alexandra. How did you know where I lived?'

'It's on Facebook. It was posted by ...Michael Bush. He was your ex-husband, wasn't he, Rose? There was something about a will reading last year for your Uncle Albert. He didn't leave you anything, but your address was shown on the will.'

Rose kept quiet, but her Spidey senses started kicking in upon the mention of her own back story. Sandy nodded. 'OK, but it's already past eight o'clock. I would rather not go through anything tonight. It would be better to meet at the Coffee Club Sherwood, eleven a.m. this Wednesday as you told me before.'

'All right then. I'm so sorry to have bothered you. I will certainly be there, and I remind you again, Rose cannot come along this time either.' The woman turned and descended the stairs.

Dog came back out and made sure she'd left. Rose and Sandy looked at each other. 'Now, that was weird.'

'Yep, Sandy and I didn't hear a car either. So, she lives around here and walks home or down to the ferry stop. Do you want to find out? Do we take a walk and follow her?'

'Nope, I don't like this at all. That's why I made it Wednesday; I think it's time to bring in the 'big guns' to have a look.'

'You mean Nic?'

'Yep.'

They rang Nic, and he answered with: *'Thank you for calling Oliver's Optometry. We can make a spectacle of anything.'*

'Hey Nic, be serious. It's us, and we think we need your help with the Alexandra Ripley thing.' There was loud music in the background. 'Sorry, I can't quite hear you. Can I ring you back in the morning?'

'Sure, it sounds like you're at a nightclub without us. What's that all about?'

'Not quite a nightclub. It's only after eight, so I'll be in touch.'

Dog sat down on the top of the stairs, gave a loud meow, and then went back inside. Rose nodded in confirmation. 'I think that means Dog doesn't like Alexandra either, and I think I'm with him on that too. My Spidey senses are telling us to be careful here. Anyway, I wonder what Nic was up to, he's usually quite excited about telling us he's having a late night, even if it's all by himself.'

Rose and Sandy decided to go back inside, binge-watch a couple of episodes of "Game of Thrones" and after discussing whether Jason Mamoa looked better in the movie Aqua Man or G.O.T., they decided the show was too hard to follow as everyone was being killed.

They retired to bed.

Meanwhile, Nic was sitting on one of the wooden bleachers on the top level of the 'Brisbane River Night Club Cruise boat, watching the woman who had just boarded at the West End Ferry terminal. His network of people had been following her for a few days. As predicted, she used the nightclub boat instead of a regular ferry to avoid travel detection from any C.C.T.V. cameras on public transport. Nic managed to take her photograph with his phone and send it to Chewy to run it through a facial recognition program.

A few minutes later, his phone pinged: 'Matched both passports.'

Alexandra moved towards a group of six well-heeled gentlemen and asked one to assist her in removing her Armani coat. They were all happy to oblige, as underneath, she wore a sheer blood-red Armani mini-skirt, and they all noticed.

Nic had wondered what Alexandra's next move would be as he hoped to watch her in action. He didn't have to wait long, as one of the silver-haired stately gentlemen had taken her aside to find a more intimate area. Nic believed it wasn't a random meeting, so he followed them to try to listen into their conversation, and eventually, she led him to a secluded cabin within the boat.

Alexandra and her beau were now sitting at one end of the small bar, and she'd shifted his hand to rest on her bare knee. 'Two hundred thousand. If you put in that, I'll pay you ten per cent. Way better than any banks or the stock market, and I even guarantee the returns.'

The man softly caressed her knee. 'What guarantee will you give me?'

'My word. I offer no more than that. If you can arrange to deposit the funds right now, I'll spend the rest of the night with you.'

The man grinned. 'All night?'

Alexandra softly tapped her hand on his face, then shifted his hand from her knee, and put it back onto the bar. 'Nope. It's not that kind of business proposal. It's just until we dock, so you have about two hours. I'm your companion, and that's all. Think of me as an expensive handbag that will make you a lot of money. Nothing more, nothing less.'

The man nodded. 'So, you'll be my new girlfriend for the two-hour boat cruise, then what happens?'

Alexandra smiled. 'If you can convince some of your other friends to invest with me, too, maybe I can think about making you all rich.' The man laughed and downed his drink.

Nic had emptied his glass well before the end of the conversation and noticed Alexandra looking over at him. 'Hey, handsome, are you looking to invest with me too?' Nic stood up and swayed a little, then sat down and responded with a hint of slurred speech. 'Only if you can get me another drunk.'

'Sure, name your poison. This is my private bar.'

'I'm partial to Macallan Single Malt but would be happy if you get me another Johnny, straight up.' Nic drew out his credit card to hand over to her, but Alexandra put her hand up to stop him. 'My shout....Mister?'

'Palmer....but don't tell anyone I'm on this cruise. I'm trying to avoid my ex-wife.'

Alexandra moved around to the back of the bar. 'OK, Mr Palmer. Johnny Red straight up it is then.' Meantime the other gentleman was a little taken aback as he had temporarily lost the opportunity to be the centre of Alexandra's attention.

'Palmer, you said. Are you in any relation to the Palmers of Brisbane?

Nic stood up, then sat down quickly, feigning an over-indulgence of liquor. 'Yep, every single one of them. Do you know of them?'

'I'm having dinner with some tomorrow night. What did you say your first name was?'

Nic stood again, pretended to sway, and quickly sat back down. 'Sshh! I didn't. My ex-wife has friends everywhere. I want a quiet night on the water, that's all.'

Alexandra grinned. 'Well, take your drink and get

out then. You can't see the water from in here anyway.' Alexandra then led Nic out of the room, handed him the drink and whispered: 'Meet me after we dock, and we'll talk about what I can offer you.'

The boat eventually returned to Eagle Street Pier, and the patrons alighted. The group of men who had been interacting with Alexandra were disappointed as she wouldn't be joining them in a late-night pub crawl. Nic waited to be one of the last ones disembarking, and Alexandra was waiting for him, dressed in the Armani coat.

'OK, then, Mr Palmer...let's go. Alchemy Restaurant has stayed open for me, and I'm sure we'll find your Macallan Single Malt there.' Alexandra took his arm, and they headed towards the restaurant, about a ten-minute walk away. Nic maintained his persona of a well-healed gentleman.

'So, tell me about yourself, Alexandra. How can you guarantee such a return in this sluggish market?' He stopped and took a breath. 'My apologies, this colder air is, um...catching up with me.'

Alexandra waited. 'You overheard that comment?'

'Yes, and I'm very interested. I've got a bunch of money coming to me, and my trader told me putting into shares seems a waste of time as there's not much action in the stock market at the moment.'

'How much is a bunch?'

'Well, can you keep a secret?'

'Try me.'

Nic leaned forward. 'I've just sold my interest in a mining business in a Western Australian diamond mine. It's worth over four hundred million dollars. I'm thinking of buying one of those private islands of The Whitsundays. I'll need to park it somewhere until I can get up there to scope things out.' Nic watched as Alexandra's face lit up.

They arrived at the restaurant, and the maître'd welcomed Alexandra like a long-lost friend. 'Welcome back again, Alexandra; so nice to join us. We have kept your table ready. Same as usual?'

Alexandra smiled, then nodded. 'Make it two Macallan Single Malts, neat. This is my friend, Mr Palmer. Please ensure we are not interrupted.'

Another couple stood up and greeted Alexandra as they passed through. Nic recognised one as a State politician, but the younger man with her was certainly not her husband. Nic knew he needed to be very careful.

They sat down, and the waiter brought over the whiskeys and then took Alexandra's coat. Alexandra raised her glass. 'To fame, fortune, getting rich and keeping secrets.'

Nic nodded, and they chinked glasses. 'Do you have any secrets, Alexandra?'

'I have a few, but my focus is tidying up loose ends. My business partners are worried about the state of the economy, so I'm seriously considering flying off into the sunset before they come after me.'

Nic nodded, and Alexandra continued: 'Only kidding, they wouldn't be able to catch me anyway. Please excuse me for a moment, as I have to say hello to some people who just came in.' Nic stood and watched her go, sat down and looked out into the night views of the Storey Bridge and Kangaroo Point.

Nic noticed someone staring back at him reflected in the glass window, then realised it was his own. His late decision to wear a disguise had paid dividends - his face was that of a stately gentleman, with wispy grey hair, a balding scalp, and the 'tattoos' of sunspots on his hands, head and face added to the illusion. He'd once stood on a stage with Alexandra whilst giving a presentation on Cyber Fraud, so continuing to be this close to her may prove a little dangerous.

Another group of people now surrounded Alexandra. Bollinger champagne was flowing freely, and she commanded their attention. 'OK, as I promised, everyone here is making substantial returns. My investments are paying dividends well beyond expectations. It's time you put your money where your mouth is and ante up some more.'

Nic took the opportunity to leave, but not before leaving a business card on their table along with a contact number on the back:

'Nique Palmer – Argyle Diamonds, Western Australia.'

CHAPTER 22

The following morning Rose and Sandy were out on the back deck having breakfast, and Dog was with them. He'd stopped eating and this time took off down the stairs. There was a cry from below; it was Nic, and he must have fallen over. 'Get this cat off me, guys. I'm trying to come up, and all it wants to do is give me a morning cuddle. I've got tofu doughnuts and hot coffee.'

Rose leaned down, shook the half-eaten bowl of kitty dins, and the cat bound up the stairs for a post-breakfast feed. Nic followed up a moment later. 'What's up, guys?'

'It's this Alexandra Ripley thing. She turned up here last night uninvited and spun some story about knowing where I lived as a copy of Uncle Albert's will is available on the net. She knew about Rose and Michael, too. We couldn't find any trace of Alexandra being at school at the same time I was, then she barked at me as she knew Rose was waiting with me in the Coffee Club. What do you think?'

Nic nodded. 'Well, Sandy, nothing means nothing

until it means something. I've spoken to Chewy about how the car was transferred over from Nic Thorn and Associates after he contacted the Sunshire Credit Union. They explained it was not part of their policy to discuss individual cases but confirmed they don't do a physical inspection of motor vehicles offered as security for a loan.'

Sandy shook her head in astonishment. 'That's unbelievable. It means I can go next door, get the details of Dave's car, ring them up, and get the loan.'

'Well, you could, but it's fraud and you'd go to jail without going past Go or collecting the two hundred dollars.'

Rose leaned forward. 'Did he find out anything else?'

'Well, have you guys heard of 'cyberstalking'? That's when people follow your online profiles, Facebook, Linked In, and Twitter and leave comments on your whereabouts. It's like using dating sites without the goofy portraits.'

Rose grinned. 'It's no wonder we stay off the internet. Did he find anything else?'

'Yep. Chewy found a lot of internet traffic on the dark web against Sandy's name, which was the easiest thing to look for: Driver's Licence, Medicare details, Tax File Number, and mother's maiden name. There were a couple of old tax returns, too. Either someone's computer has been hacked, or they've gathered it together and posted it to the dark web. Do you use an Accountant? You might want to check with them.'

'Can we find out where she lives and call in the Police?'

Nic shook his head: 'It's not that easy. Anyway, all that information is what the fraudsters use to open Bank Accounts, and from there, they can get a loan, and that's when we call the Fraud Squad.'

'OK, it all sounds so stupid...but where to from here?'

Nic nodded. 'Well, how about a little bit of sight-seeing? Have either of you been to Russell Island lately?'

Rose kept quiet, and Sandy responded. 'Nope, not for years. Have you planned a day trip with a pick-a-nick basket and everything?'

'Sure have, and I've put some hiking gear into a backpack, too. We'll take the car to Redland Bay and catch the ferry over. It's about a twenty-minute boat ride.'

Rose took a breath. 'And why the hiking gear?'

'We'll do a little walk through the National Park, ride on a couple of ATVs, do some bush bashing....that sort of thing.'

Rose nodded. 'I've heard there's a place called Melomy's Wetland. It was where the last reported sighting of a Thorn Bud Warbler was. It has a very distinct mating call like: 'Brackagh, brackagh.''

Nic struggled to stop himself from laughing.

About three hours later, the group was having brunch at The Bay View Café when a woman approached them dressed in dark navy blue cargo pants with a matching polo shirt and heavy-duty hiking boots. Nic stood up, they did a back-slapping thing and then shook hands. 'Good to see you over here again, Nic. Once you're finished here, we'll be heading down to Melomy's to have a look at the thing you want to see.'

Rose smiled. 'What thing would that be then, Nic?'

Nic took a breath. 'Just a thing that's been needing to be looked at.' Sandy was momentarily captivated by their guest, then looked at Nic. 'Nic, I thought you looked at stuff, liked finding stuff and losing stuff, not looking at...things.'

Nic shook his head. 'Nope. We're definitely looking at a thing. There might be some stuff we need to look at too, but it's definitely a thing this time. Anyway, guys, this is 'Sarge', and she'll be our guide today.' Sandy stood up and shook her hand. 'Hi, I'm Sandy. You look like a superhero dressed in civvies.'

Sarge grinned, removed her cap, and then ran her hand through a strawberry-blonde buzz cut. 'Not quite. I was never one for that type of excitement. Anyway, have you guys ridden an ATV before? I've got access to a couple of RZR Polaris. They're two-seaters. Who wants to ride with whom?'

Sandy nodded. 'I'll go with Nic, seeing Rose spent

the other day flying with him, although you guys never actually said where you went.'

Rose took a sip of her coffee. 'Over to you, Nic.'

'I would tell you, Sandy, but I can't remember. I'm nearly forty, you know.'

The group moved outside, and a Sarge led them to a white Holden Colorado 4 x 4, four-door utility. It looked like a Police Wagon without the blue stripes and light bar across the top.

Sandy climbed into the rear seat. 'This looks like a Police Car.'

Sarge nodded. 'Good to know. It might be one day when it grows up.'

They headed directly south, and after about a ten-minute drive, Sarge stopped the car, and they climbed out. Two Polaris ATVs were parked at the entrance gate to the wetlands, and Rose noticed the keys were in the ignition. 'Not much crime here on the island then, Sarge?'

'We have our good days and our bad days. Why do you ask?'

'You said we. Are you with the Police then?'

'With the Police, no. Am the Police, yes.'

Rose looked at Nic. 'So Nic, you've brought in Sarge to help us look at the thing, is there anything else we need to know?' Meantime, Nic had started the engine of his Polaris and tapped at his ear. 'I can't hear you...'

After a wet and muddy ride, the group arrived at the shed where Rose and Nic had been two days ago.

Sandy climbed out and looked around. 'Are we supposed to be going into this? Surely, it's breaking and entering and a little illegal.'

Sarge extracted a black wallet, then flipped out a Police badge: 'Senior Sargeant Phillipa Sargeant, nice to formally meet you. Nic has told me a lot about his two associates and it's nice to put names to faces.' Sarge then whispered to Rose: 'Although you did see me here yesterday.'

Rose nodded. 'Where?'

Sarge smiled. 'I think you saw me at the window of the shed.'

Rose shook her head. 'So, you've already been here and seen what's inside. What do you think? Are we onto something illegal here?'

'I would say so, but we still don't know what it is. There are a lot of things to go through; the least of all is trying to find out who owns everything.'

They moved towards the large building, and Sarge raised her hand to indicate the group should stop, and Nic handed him the monocular. Sarge did a quick scan. 'It looks like the cameras are now in use. Can you do something about that?'

Nic pulled his phone out and messaged Chewy. 'Cameras?' The response came back quickly: **Wi-Fi down ATM. Good to go.** Nic gave the all-clear. 'The network is down at the moment. Chewy will let me know if it comes back on and we have to get out quickly.'

Sandy was still trying to work out what was going on between Rose, Sarge and Nic and if it was legal to enter the shed, even if they were with the Police. Sarge then knocked loudly on the door and announced:

'Under Queensland Law, I am legally authorised to commence a search on the basis where I believe there is evidence on these premises that may be destroyed or compromised. Please identify yourself if you are present.'

There was no response. 'Over to you, Nic.'

Nic nodded and tried 0000 on the lock, but it didn't open this time. Sarge stood there waiting, so Nic tried again, then kicked the door, and it yielded after the fourth attempt. 'That will work. Good job.'

They stepped inside, and Rose noticed quite a number of the crates and cases had been removed. The triple whiteboard was also gone, along with the filing cabinet.

Rose sighed. 'This isn't good, is it?'

Sarge nodded. 'It looks like they're already on the move. I'll get the Brisbane Crime Squad over here later today, but in the meantime let's look for something that might contain D.N.A. - it could be a discarded tissue or a water bottle.'

The group searched for over an hour, and Sarge had enough. 'OK. Let's finish up. My guys aren't able to come over until tomorrow.'

In the meantime, Nic had been scouring the plane for anything and called out from the back area. 'I've got something here. The pilot stored the flight folder underneath the passenger seat. They must have missed it.' Nic extracted it carefully and went to place it into an evidence bag.

Sarge came over. 'Wait. Let's have a look to see who's been flying it.'

They found a table and placed the log book down. 'I can't quite make out the name. It looks like Nelson Torres.'

Nic called Chewy. 'Nelson Torres? OK good. Thanks.' Nic looked up. 'Chewy has found a Nelson Torres. He is a senior partner with an accounting practice in Brisbane. It might be worth checking him out and could explain how they're washing the money through the system. He's also a pilot. Got to love Facebook.'

Meanwhile, Rose and Sandy stepped back outside to wait for the others. Nic and Sarge came out, and Sarge secured the door with an official Police lock, then crisscrossed it with the blue Police tape. Sandy looked at the patchwork across the door. 'I've always wondered how that works as a defence?'

Sarge smiled. 'It doesn't stop them from going in, but they can't go in without breaking it. All secure here, Nic.'

Nic and Sarge then climbed some nearby trees to set up their camera network, and Nic was halfway up a tree when he felt something wet hitting his arm. 'Damn, I think a koala has just peed on me.'

Rose looked up. 'I don't think so as this island doesn't have any koalas.'

'Well, something just peed on me.'

Sarge called up from further up the tree. 'Sorry, it was me.'

'Err...thanks, Sarge.'

'But don't worry, it was only from my water bottle.'

They dropped from the trees and climbed back onto the ATVs, and Nic called Chewy again and then addressed the group. 'Our cameras are working, but the wi-fi is a bit sketchy. We might not see anything anyway.'

They rode back to the Colorado, then drove to the café for late lunch.

They were now waiting at the ferry to return to the mainland when Rose took a moment with Sarge. 'If you were already in the shed when we came in, why didn't you let us know?'

'Um...I came in via the skylight on the roof. I had to break the lock to get in, so technically, it's breaking and entering, which might be against the law. I was hiding in the runabout. Nic knew I was there. I spoke to him a few days ago to let him know I'd found the plane and a whole lot of other suspect stuff.'

Rose shook her head. 'How long have you been watching the place?'

'About a month. Not much exciting stuff happens on the island, so when Nic told me about this setup, it gave me something interesting to look into.'

Rose looked at her. 'If Nic has known about it for a month, I suspect he knows about Alexandra Ripley, too.'

Sarge shrugged. 'You'll have to ask him.'

CHAPTER 23

It was early morning and Rose and Sandy were again sitting on their deck watching Dog tormenting a miniature schnauzer by tempting it to come closer towards his bowl of kitty dins. The little dog assumed no one was around to prevent it from gaining access, so when Dog finally came out from his hiding place, the poor little dog got the fright of its little life and scampered off, yelping to anyone listening.

Nic rang the doorbell, so they brought him in, and together, they sat in the lounge room. 'If you are OK with it, I'd like to wire you up with a recorder for your meeting this morning with Alexandra. We'll record the conversation in case she incriminates herself, and if you see an older couple arguing, ignore them, as it might be Rose and me in disguise.'

Sandy nodded. 'Sure. Remember the meeting is at eleven. Do you want me to try and get a selfie with her, too?'

'Nup. Leave it all to us.'

'Will it be just Rose and you?'

'Not just us. I will have others from my team there,

too. I'm getting a feeling about this woman. You've already met my bug guy as he did the bug-guy-sweep when we found the mini cameras.'

'Anything else, Nic.'

'Yes, well, it was pretty brazen of her to come here. Can you describe her to me?'

'Average height. Average weight. Blonde hair, maybe brown underneath, as her eyebrows were darker. Brown eyes. Maybe a size eight to ten. Wore blue jeans and a white shirt. She was a local, as the way she spoke was Queensland-ish. What does it matter? Surely you will see her today?'

'Yep, but what if someone else turns up? It was dark last night when she came here.'

Sandy nodded. 'Gee, you're paranoid.'

'Yep, to that too. I've been doing this a long time and got beaten up once by a guy who turned out to be someone else. I thought he was a mate, but he had an older brother. I was going out with a girl that the brother had a crush on.'

'How long ago was that?'

'About twenty-seven years.'

'That makes you about ten years old when it happened.'

'I know. It's put me off from dating ever since. That was until I used the Vita Brevis app and hooked up with Rose.'

'You told Carly you'd only used it once.'

'Yep, that's true. Dating is just so complicated.'

Rose and Sandy shook their heads. 'And now you have double trouble with us.' Nic nodded. 'Anyhow, let's get this thing started. We'll see you at the Coffee Club, but remember, don't look for us.'

Rose and Nic drove off to Bowen Hills to don their disguises, and Dave hobbled up the stairs. 'Hey Sandy, are you meeting with Alexandra again?'

'Yes, this morning. Nic and Rose will be there too.'

'Did you want me to come along as well?'

'I don't think so, but thanks anyway.'

'I'll come along as your friend if you want. She's already met me so I won't be a face she doesn't know.'

'OK. I'll think about it. Can I use your car again? Nic hasn't been able to get the Peugeot back for us, and I don't want to drive our car. It's too old and too small.'

'OK, but only if you let me come along.'

'All right, I'll let Nic know.'

'Fine, see you about ten.'

Sandy called Nic. 'Dave wants to come too. He's already met, Alexandra. Is that OK?'

'Sure, but tell him to stay in the car. Has my guy turned up to wire you up?'

'Yes, he apologised as I had to unbutton my shirt. He kept looking the other way, and at one stage, I had to hold his hands against my chest to ensure the wires were secured properly.'

'OK. I'll give him a few days off to recover.'

It was now 10.25 a.m., and Sandy had been fussing about it. Dog had been fed at least five times and she finally decided to collect Dave, but he didn't appear to be home. Sandy knew the spare key, so they unlocked the door and went inside. The place had been ransacked, so I immediately called Nic.

'What's up?'

'Dave's missing. His place is a mess, and it looks like he's been robbed. Should I call the Police?'

Nic went quiet. 'Nope, not yet. Come alone, then. See you in about half an hour.'

Sandy arrived at the Sherwood Coffee Club just before 11 a.m., and Alexandra was already waiting. 'Hi, Sandy. I'm glad you could make it this time, and it looks like you convinced your neighbour not to come.'

Sandy considered the comment regarding Dave not attending but decided not to press the issue. 'What's this about, Alexandra?'

'Well, for a start, you can call me Sandy.'

'I won't do that. Did you go to school with me?'

'What do you think?'

'No, but why are you doing this to me?'

'Sandy, Sandy. You took away my little Bank man at the Community Bank, and I was onto a good thing, too. I had already taken a mortgage on your place and needed access to some more money. I have some bad people whom I owe money to. I saw the house title particulars on that paper deed in your den and took my opportunity. I was supposed to watch you with those stupid little cameras, but your stupid man Nic Thorn discovered them. I want to meet him again one day and personally thank him for making me change my plans.'

Sandy didn't know how to react. 'I'm not going to call you Sandy, as that's my name, and you disrespect it. Should I call you Alex or something else?'

'I don't care, Sandy. I need the money, and you will help me get it. We're going to take a walk across the road to the Community Bank. We will meet with the Loan Manager as he has some documents for you to sign, and then you're to transfer the money into my account with the Sunshire Credit Union. You are buying a house for a friend.'

'What if I refuse?'

'Dave, your neighbour, won't be happy as his house might get burnt down. He told me he couldn't join you today as he is tied up.' The woman laughed at her statement. 'All tied up underneath his house.' Sandy was about to say something else, but an argument had started between an elderly couple at the following table. Sandy smiled, and Alexandra noticed. 'Why are you smiling, Sandy? Is it because that couple is your friend Rose and Nic dressed up in disguises? They look like the old couple from the Banking seminar thing at South Bank a few months ago.'

Sandy glared at Alexandra. 'Right, you were the woman on the stage, weren't you? You said the thing about loan fraud is a victimless crime. That's just stupid, Alexandra. We pay higher interest rates on Credit Cards and home loans. Besides that, you'll go to jail this time as you'll be arrested. I'll have them add a charge of butchering the ABBA song, 'Money, Money, Money', that you sang too.'

Alexandra stood up, went over to the elderly couple, picked up the salt cellar and slammed it back down in front of the face of the elderly man. The old woman screamed and went to the aid of her husband. 'John, John, are you OK?' Alexandra grabbed the old woman by the shoulders and pressed her onto the chair. 'Sit down, you stupid cow.'

Sandy realised that the arguing couple wasn't Nic and Rose, and wondered where they were. It was all getting a little serious.

Alexandra leaned into the couple, 'Listen to me, you morons, take the salt or don't take the salt. No one else cares or wants to hear your stupid argument.'

Sandy went to stand up. 'Yes, Sandy, get up. You're coming with me right now as we're going over the road to the Bank. Our appointment is in five minutes.'

Alexandra and Sandy left the elderly couple quivering in her wake, crossed the road at a pedestrian crossing, and went straight into the banking chamber of the Community Bank. Alexandra led Sandy into one of the open offices, then shut the door, where a portly-looking, ruddy-cheeked loan arranger was waiting behind the desk. The Banker looked up and smiled.

Alexandra held out her hand and sat down, then beckoned Sandy to join her. 'Hello, I'm Alexandra

Ripley, and this is my friend, Sandra Fraser. We have an appointment with you to sign some loan documents. Sandra is buying a house for me. Isn't that nice of her? Sandra has read through the Pre-Contractual Loan Agreement you sent her Post Box. So, we are ready to sign.'

The man stood up, shook their hands, and spoke with a hint of a New Zealand accent. 'Muss Fraser and Muss Ripley. Thank you so very much for coming un. This loan was dun over the unternit. It's all approved and uverything. I need to chuck some details. Do you have your driver's Licence, Muss Fraser?'

Sandy looked at Alexandra. 'Yes,' however, Alexandra pulled it from her pocket and handed it to him.

The Banker nodded. 'Thank you. I'll just take a snippy picture with my phone, we must do this for VOI, sorry, 'bank jargon.' It's Verification Of Identification. Do you have any questions, Muss Fraser, before we sign?'

Alexandra interjected. 'No, she doesn't, Mister...um, sorry we didn't catch your name?' The Banker smiled. 'Ok, sorry, Muss Ripley. Mr Crow, Ross Crow.' Alexandra looked at him. 'I know that name. Have we met before?'

'Oh, no, I'm only new here. Left my last job as a smull Hotel Manager only recently. He sacked me because I threw a phone at him.'

Alexandra continued: 'Right, let's get this done then, Mr Crow. There is already a mortgage over the property, so it's just a matter of Sandra signing the loan application and the form to disburse the money.'

'That's right, so where are we putting the money thun?'

'It's going directly to my Bank Account with Sunshire Credit Union and Mr Crow, I will be able to access the funds straight away, won't I?'

'Yus, as the sun as I get the forms signed, the money will go out pronto. You can watch it all huppen, too. It's all dun here on my computer.'

Sandy looked at the Loan Manager, smiled, signed the forms, and she felt a tear welling in her eye.

The Bank man processed the loan, then turned the computer screen towards them to see the money had been transferred.

Alexandra looked at the screen, then logged into the Sunshire Credit Union via her phone and confirmed the transfer. 'Thank you so very much. Mister Crow. We'll be going now.'

'Well, thank you for your customers too in fuct we have a small presentation for you both outside. Congratulations, you're my hundredth loan customer.' The Banker stood up, opened the door, and Sandy gave the banker a light kiss on the cheek when passing him. 'Thank you for your help, Mr Crow.'

Alexandra stepped out and noticed the elderly couple from the Coffee Club were now in the Banking chamber. 'That is you, Nic 'Stupid' Thorn? And I see you're with your stupid girlfriend, Rose.'

The elderly couple looked back at her and quickly turned away.

Sandy interjected. 'I don't think so, Alexandra, that isn't Nic and Rose.'

The two women then made their way towards the exit, and another portly, ruddy-cheeked Loan Manager came out from another office. He stood at the front door and was dressed almost like the other banker.

Alexandra laughed at them. 'Who are you both supposed to be? Tweedle Dumb, and Tweedle Dumber?'

There was a voice from behind her. 'No, I'm Nic 'stupid' Thorn, and that is Miss Palmer standing by the door. Stop, Alexandra, the party is over.'

Alexandra weighed her options, darted for the door and barrelled directly into Rose. 'Get out of my way, you stupid fat cow.' They wrestled a little and she managed to manoeuvre Rose out of the way, then she stepped outside and began singing the ABBA song, '*Money, money, money...*'

Alexandra then dashed across the pedestrian crossing, but collided heavily with an oncoming car, bounced off the bonnet and landed in a crumpled heap on the road. The car screeched to a stop.

Rose and Sandy rushed to her, and the driver jumped out. He removed a crash helmet and hobbled up to them. 'She doesn't look too good; she might have a broken arm and a broken leg. We can only hope.' They all looked down at the crumpled woman, and Sandy smiled. 'You can bank on that.'

The group looked back at the crumpled car - it had suffered major damage. The roof and bonnet were caved in, the windscreen smashed, and the left front wheel no longer pointed forward.

Dave looked at Sandy. 'Sorry about your little Nissan S-Cargo. It bore the brunt of the collision. You might not be able to drive it again.'

Meantime, a small crowd had gathered around, and the Police soon arrived to review the scene. Dave continued: 'Nic gave me the signal she was coming out, so I had to line her up perfectly. I was only allowed to bring her down, not to kill her. Nic doesn't allow that sort of thing. Who knew?'

Sandy smiled again. 'We did.'

Nic waddled up to the group, peeling off his disguise. 'I do have some good news, guys. The Peugeot will be delivered back to you later today, and Sandy, when exactly did you know it was me in there.'

Sandy looked at him. 'Ross Crow? Throwing a shoe, come on. I thought she would've seen through it straight away. Maybe it was your silly attempt at a New Zealand accent that threw her?'

Nic nodded. 'I know. I only had a couple of hours to put it together, too. Lucky Rose didn't speak. I had no idea what accent she'd been working on.'

Rose looked at them. 'Dahlings, have you seen my Gladiola's anywhere?'

They looked at her and Rose continued. 'Hey, if Barry Humphries can get away with being dressed up as Dame Edna Everidge, at least I can do is talk like her.'

Dave shook his head. 'But you're dressed as a man.'

'Oops, I forgot.'

The Ambulance arrived, and Alexandra was loaded onto the gurney. The Police handcuffed her and then followed the vehicle to the hospital. Sandy watched the Ambulance leave, but the account transfer still concerned her. 'Nic, how do I get my money back? I don't get it; if the money went into her account, I now have a loan. I saw it in there.'

'Yep, it did, but she was never going to be able to take it out. They'd put a stop to any withdrawals. It will be reversed from the account, and the loan here will be negated.'

Dave tapped the crash helmet. 'Can we go home now? I need a shower and a cold beer, and I have a bit of a headache. I'm your friendly neighbourhood neighbour, not a Hollywood stuntman.'

CHAPTER 24

A few days later, Rose, Sandy and Dave were having drinks and a hot chicken lunch on Sandy's rear deck at West End. They were taking turns throwing chicken titbits to Dog. Nic came up the stairs to join them, and he went over the latest developments since Alexandra's arrest:

'She'd been on the Police radar for over three years, but they needed to catch her in the act. She's been using several false passports, including that of Sandy Fraser and Alexandra Ripley. It was probably how she got so far with your stolen ID. They are in the process of shutting down a major Ponzi scheme, too.'

Sandy added. 'And she confessed to me she was the woman who gave the little song and dance routine at the Australian Banking Association seminar a few months ago. We missed our chance then.'

'Not really, Sandy. We had no idea she was the same person doing everything.' Sandy sighed. 'I guess so. Anyway, Dave, how did you get caught, then untied?'

'Well, it's a bit embarrassing. Alexandra told me your cat had chased her little sausage dog under my house, so I did the chivalrous thing and helped her look, then she walloped me with something and tied me up. That's the last time I help out a damsel in distress, never again, until next time anyway.'

'But how did you get untied?'

'The Postman untied me. He's scared of Dog, so as he was delivering the mail, Dog rounded him up and herded him towards me laying underneath the house.'

Rose smiled. 'So, did Dog untie you?'

'Nope, the Postman. He heard me crying out for help, then I rang Nic.'

'What about the car? What made you think of using that as a weapon?'

'That was Rose's idea.'

'Sorry, Sandy. I thought it was time we retired the old girl and decided to take it out with a bang. I hope you don't mind.'

'Nope, we can claim it on our Insurance policy. It was damaged in the normal course of business.' Nic had overheard the comment. 'Sorry, Sandy, but that sounds like an Insurance scam.'

'Damn you, Nic.' Rose interjected. 'Hey, that's my line.'

Dave hobbled off, and Nic started to leave, but his phone rang, so he sat back down. 'OK. Thanks for letting me know. That's interesting. I wouldn't have thought she'd be doing that. She's still being charged and everything. Thanks again, Sarge, see you here in about twenty minutes.' Nic hung up.

Rose looked over. 'What's up?'

'Sarge has been with the Fraud Squad linking it all together. They tracked down the previous owner of the Sea Plane, and it turns out it was stolen. He flew it from Cairns down to Caboolture to donate it to their museum, met with a woman called Myra Duquesne, and handed it over. Two days later, he went back to see if everything was OK, and they said, 'Plane .... what plane?'

'So, they're getting it back?'

'Yep, and also, the Queensland Surf Life Saving people are about to receive a donation of five brand new jet skis. Just in time for summer.'

There was a knock on the door, and Sandy answered it. It was Sarge, and she wore the same attire they'd seen him with on Russell Island. She nodded at the group and Sandy invited her inside to make a coffee for her. Sarge to a sip.

'Good coffee. So, Sandy, can I ask you a question about Nic?'

Sandy nodded. 'Sure, but I don't know much about him. Rose has known him for about five hours more than me.'

'No actually, it's about you and Nic.'

'You mean...Rose and me and Nic?'

'Um...I'm not sure what that means. I just wanted to know your um...status with you and Nic.'

'Oh, right. We both work for him.'

'What about other stuff?'

'That's about it.'

'Good to know.'

Sandy didn't quite understand where the conversation was going, so she led Sarge through the house and onto the rear deck. Sarge nodded to all, then updated them: 'Well, our little ID scammer lady had put together a dossier on the three of you. We'd found incriminating evidence concerning the fraudulent loans she was involved in, and you were being set up as her accomplices.'

Nic smiled. 'What sort of stuff did she have on us?'

'She'd been using those little cameras to collect your conversations.'

Nic nodded this time. 'Interesting. I'll need to check what my geek guy did. He told me he'd neutralised them.'

Rose responded. 'Oh, no, just what did she overhear?'

Sarge shook her head and continued, 'A bit of this, a bit of that, but she was collecting your voice samples and compiling a sound bite to imply you were all part of her ID fraud team.'

Nic took over. 'Lucky, we grabbed her when we did. I didn't want to explain what I do to Sarge's people higher up the chain of command, they might think I'm crazy for doing what I do.'

Rose grinned. 'What's new? Everyone thinks you're crazy putting up with us.'

Sarge added. 'Good to know. Anyway, we took a

little visit to the accountancy practice. It's called 'Best Accounting Group'. We met with a junior partner named Michael Bush. He denied having anything to do with anything.'

Rose looked at him. 'Michael Bush...about yay high, roundish face that matches his roundish head and roundish shape.' Sarge nodded, and Rose continued. 'He was my ex-husband. We were married for three days. Serve him right if he's got anything to do with this.'

'Nope, sorry, that was his point. The senior partner, Nelson Torres, had just been marched from the premises that morning, and this Bush guy was representing the practice as a senior proxy partner. All the other partners were off on a junket somewhere. Bush was quite helpful though and let us into Torres' office without a warrant or anything.'

Nic smiled. 'Did you get a look at Torres' computer?'

'Yes, Bush even let us look through his computer. He told me their internal security protocols don't allow the sharing of passwords, but somehow he knew it.'

Rose nodded. 'I wouldn't put it past Michael that he'd collected other stuff on all the senior partners. He'd be using it to get a promotion if the opportunity ever raised itself.'

Sarge nodded and pulled from her briefcase a folder. 'Good to know, anyway he printed off the dossier for me to review, and here it is.' Sarge opened the folder and splayed it across the table. It showed a list of Nelson Torres' known associates, including Alexandra Ripley/Myra Duquesne. Michael had added a note suspecting she was the same person and Torres was lodging a false insurance claim about a stolen seaplane. There was also a photograph of her taken at a local bakery, having met with Torres and handing him a brown paper bag.

The files also contained a list of times when Torres had visited the local Community Bank in Brisbane and other notes taken from the banking staff. There was even a diary showing when and where Michael had been questioning them about what Torres had been doing. The bags contained cash and were deposited into a business bank account under 'Got 2 Getaway Pty Ltd'.

Nic smiled. 'This is very thorough.'

Sarge nodded. 'Oh, it gets better.' She flicked through the file and pulled out photocopies of the AUSTRAC declarations made by banking staff.'

Sandy leaned forward. 'I thought they only recorded cash deposits over ten thousand.'

Nic shook his head. 'Nope, Any cash deposit can be recorded under another form called 'Suspicious Activity Report' or an SMR. Banks are obligated to report any significant cash deposit, even if it is legitimate, like a cash sale of a car. It's where the cash originated that piques AUSTRAC interest.'

Rose stood up, sighed, and stood by the balcony. 'I guess I have to give Michael his dues then. He's made the case to prosecute so much easier. Did he show you any other files?'

Sarge nodded. 'I found another one. Bush had left the room to make a phone call, so I went through the filing cabinet. I didn't know if he'd left it unlocked deliberately.' Sarge closed the Torres file and laid the second file on the table. It was labelled 'Nic Thorn and Associates.' It contained information about when and where Nic first met with Rose and Sandy. There were notes from the will reading information and how often Rose is away from home.

Sarge nodded. 'This guy is still hung up on you, isn't he?'

Rose sighed. 'Yes, unfortunately, even after a ten-year marriage to Dimond and two children later. He still thinks he's in with a chance with me.'

Nic read a few more notes from the file, closed it and put it under his arm. 'How unfortunate, this file was destroyed in a shredder. If it was never here, did it ever exist at all? If a bear sits in the woods, was it ever there at all?'

Rose looked at him and shook her head. 'In the office, first door on the right.' Nic and Sandy walked back into the house, and Rose heard the grinding sound of paper through a shredder.

Sarge leaned forward. 'So Rose, you and Nic have known each other for a few years?'

'Nope, only about ten months. We hooked up on a dating site. He turned up in a white Mustang with a bouquet of Lisianthus and swept me off my feet. Well, at least to my Uncle Albert's funeral, and to the wake afterwards and ever since. We follow him around Australia busting scammers and looking into frauds.'

'Right.... what's your background then? P. I's, the Service? What about Sandy?'

Rose smiled. 'No, we both ran a couture business at Hamilton. It closed down when they put the new road through. As for Sandy, she's known Nic for about five hours less than me. She met him at the wake.'

'Good to know.'

'You say that a lot.'

'Yes.... Well, it is good to know about stuff and things.'

Sandy and Nic returned empty-handed. 'Job done. What's next?'

Sarge sat there thinking, then finally looked up. 'Would you like to visit Myra Duquesne, formerly known as Alexandra Ripley? I saw her this morning at the Royal Brisbane Hospital. She is still under guard, but I'm sure she'd love to meet you all again.'

Sandy rubbed her hands together. 'Great, let me get my whip.'

They watched her go back inside, and about fifteen minutes later, Sandy returned dressed as Wonder Woman, including a black wig, with Dog in tow dressed in an armoured suit. 'It may not be a Lasso of Truth, but I'm sure if you leave us alone with her for ten minutes, I can get something out of her. If not me, Dog will.'

Nic shook his head. 'Sorry, Sandy-Diana-Prince. I don't think you're allowed to take animals into the hospital, the whip maybe, but not Dog.'

'Are you sure?'

Sarge nodded. 'I can get you in. The Canteen Cancer guys in the hospital are always looking for more superheroes to perk up the kids.'

They left Dog at home and headed for the hospital. Sandy and Rose went in the Peugeot, and Sarge took Nic in the Colorado. They parked the cars, and Sarge put an 'Active Police Business' sign on the dashboard. Nic pointed it out to Rose, alluding that he once used a similar sign in his car. 'See it works.'

'But Nic, you're not the Police.'

Nic shook his head. 'Details, details....why bother with the details.'

The group headed towards the ward where Alexandra was stationed, and Sarge stopped them at the door. It read, 'Only one visitor at a time, please.' Sandy was nominated to go in first, rolling the whip through her hands as she went in. 'Hello, Alexandra or Myra or whatever you call yourself. You're not a Sandy, and I'm here to discover the truth and nothing but the truth, so help me, Dog.'

The nurse, dressed in a full face mask and blue coverall, held her hand up to stop Sandy from getting closer to the bed. 'I'm sorry, she's asleep, and I'm not going to wake her. She's been through an awful lot, being run down by a crazed motorist and all that.'

Sandy sighed, turned, left the room, and went outside the door to join the others. 'The nurse said she's asleep. Sarge, surely, with your Police powers of persuasion, you can wake her up for an informal interview?'

Sarge nodded. 'I'll see what I can do.'

Sarge went in and came back almost immediately. 'Well, the patient is not asleep... she's wide awake and very angry.'

Sandy smiled. 'Good.'

'Actually, it's not good. The nurse is tied up in the bed, and our prisoner has just leapt from the first-storey window to make her escape.'

They entered the ward, helped untie the nurse, removed the surgical gauze from across her mouth and unwrapped the bindings. 'She trumped me...never in my day have I had that. I was washing her, and she asked me to unclip the handcuffs to make it easier for her to roll over. She assured me she wouldn't try to escape.'

Sandy pulled at the last of the tape from the nurse's wrist. 'I guess she lied.'

The group looked out of the open window and caught a glimpse of a woman in blue running across the lanes of traffic heading up the road towards the Victoria Park Golf Course.

Nic took a breath. 'Well, at least we know her legs

are OK. She's got about five minutes on us.' Sarge looked out the open window, then down at the drop below. 'What do you say a nice tuck and roll when we land?'

Nic nodded. 'Yep.'

Nic went first, landed, tucked, and rolled, then Sarge followed, and they were off and running. Rose looked down at them. 'I guess that means we take the stairs and get the car.'

Rose and Sandy moved quickly through the hospital to their car and caught up with Nic and Sarge, running up the street within a few minutes. Rose beeped the horn, and they climbed in.

Nic had hardly broken a sweat. 'She's in good shape. I hate running after people that don't want to get caught.' Sarge took a few deep breaths 'I would be running too if I was trying not to get caught and lose access to about three million dollars. The Fraud Team have only scratched the surface so far. It appears she's got her tentacles in many pies, and there will be some very annoyed people.'

Sandy turned around. 'A genuine Ponzi scheme, then?'

'Yes, and many other fraud stuff, including your loan. She kept the money flowing back to the investors using fraudulently borrowed money. Some of the statements for the bank loans were going to Nelson Torres's office, so it all appeared legitimate. The Fraud guys have found a folder on his computer showing all the names. It's quite a large operation.'

Sandy grinned. 'And we brought it all down in a couple of days.'

Nic was quietly watching for the escapee when he yelled out. 'Take a hard right, Rose. She's on the Golf Course. The second hole, I think.'

Rose turned the wheel and the car bounced over the kerb. They drove over the green fairway, much to the annoyance of a pair of golfers trying to set up for their shot. Sandy lowered her window. 'Fore.'

Nic called out between bounces. 'Make that one. I think she's about to stop running or change direction.'

Alexandra slowed her gait and headed into the large Driving Range enclosure and through the open gate into the internal perimeter fence area. The tractor driver on the ball-collector machine was donning a helmet, baseball face mask, and armoured suit. He was oblivious to her entry. Nic directed Rose to slow down. 'At least she's stuck in the cage now. One large cage that usually traps wayward golf balls, and not hospital escapees.'

Rose pulled the car to a stop.

Nic and Sarge leapt out and followed their quarry through the open gate. Once through, however, they ran in the opposite direction, heading instead towards a grassy tableau where the Golf Professional was undertaking a lesson to five people. Golf balls flew everywhere, and Nic and Sarge did their best to avoid the incoming missiles.

Rose reversed the car and drove to the carpark, then they ran through the Pro Shop, hoping to catch up with the others. Meantime, Nic and Sarge had casually joined the lesson. They'd each selected their weapon, albeit a golf iron, and were watching Alexandra cowering on one side of the field, trapped by the myriad of wayward balls.

'What you say, Nic, about one fifty? A nice five iron might be the right choice.' Sarge put a ball down and swung, and the ball landed about a metre from her feet.

'A little to the right, Sarge.'

Sarge put down the next ball and made the shot. This one hit the mesh fence just above Alexandra, who was either trying to determine whether the incoming missiles were deliberate, or how to climb the fence. Nic had noticed the ball retrieval tractor coming in from the side gate and decided that might be a better alternative for her capture. He ran down, jumped on, and then directed the operator to drive to Alexandra.

Nic jumped off as the tractor moved closer, held her up against the fence, and handcuffed her. Alexandra started calling out despite the suspicious increase of golf balls heading their way.

'You can't arrest me. You're not the Police. Let me go. Help, help.'

Nic ignored her pleas, sat her on the front of the

tractor, and they headed back to the front of the driving range where Sarge was now waiting. Some golfers had since noticed a moving target, so they took pot-shots at the tractor and the two people riding in the front. Nic signalled to the driver to stop, and he stood up.

'It's OK, everyone, she's a runaway from a Hen's night.' He held up the cuffs, and the golfers cheered.

Sarge took her into custody, and a half hour later, the Fraud Squad arrived at the Golf Course to collect their prisoner. This time, they took her directly to jail without passing go.

A few hours later, Nic's group was at Irish Murphy's on George Street, not far from the Police station, waiting for Sarge. She had stayed in the watchhouse to finalise the paperwork and promised to catch up with them later. Nic took a long sip of his celebratory glass of Guinness. 'You know how I keep promising to take you overseas? I hope your passports are up to date.'

Sandy leaned. 'Yes. Rose and I did that months ago. What have you got for us?'

'The Department of Agriculture and Fisheries has confirmed we can investigate illegal reptile and bird transportation. It starts up in Cairns, then onto Fiji.'

Rose nodded. 'And?'

'Well, guys, we'll be looking into genuine budgie smugglers.'

Thanks to Plastic Bertrand for providing the words of Ca Plane Pour Moi. (Rose, that's French for 'thanks for pouring my drink') (No, Nic, it means, 'I don't want to be part of your stupid plans.')

Keep reading for an excerpt from the next adventure in the Nic Thorn Caper Series: 'Four Brooding Birds.'

Four Brooding Birds

Rosemary Palmer was surrounded by guano. She was working as a volunteer at the Greater Animal Life Zoo just outside Cairns, Far North Queensland. Nic Thorn, her business partner and mentor, had promised no more crap jobs. She had a shovel in one hand and her face mask in the other. Rose wiped her brow, raised her 1.7m frame, and stretched. 'This is back-breaking work, Sandy.' Her BFF Sandy Fraser was taking the latest full wheelbarrow away; she stopped and looked back. 'Yep, Nic lied to us, Rose.'

'I know. He'd promised to be whisking us away on an all-expense paid overseas trip to investigate the latest scam. He even made sure our passports were up to date too, but now has us shovelling bird poo instead.'

'It could be worse, Rose. This morning, I was talking to one of the other volunteers. It's her roster this week to attend to the hippo enclosure. Did you know hippos mark their territory by flicking their scat around? When they have to ...they start twirling their tails like a fan. It sprays everywhere.'

'OK. Thanks for the tip, and that's one animal enclosure I'll avoid. Besides, have you seen Nic? And what's this one all about? He'd said something about looking into budgie smugglers. Spare the thought.'

'I've been reading up on it, Rose. A group of people get their kicks by catching Australian reptiles and birds, stuffing them in cooking pots or plastic tubes and shipping them overseas. The Department of Agriculture and Fisheries has brought in Nic and his Associates to check it out. Speaking of checking things out and of the devil himself, here comes Nic.'

Nic ambled over, dressed in the uniform of the Australian Border Police. His dark, brooding looks and 1.9m frame appear very imposing. He had a stern look on his face, a look of complete focus. Then he smiled at them, and Rose shook her head. 'Wow, Nic. Whilst we are shovelling birdsh… You get all prettied up and handsomely dressed as Major Catastrophe.'

'Now that's not fair, Rose. Someone has to be a chief, and someone has to be the Indians. You know the poop. Oops, sorry guys, wrong choice of words.'

Sandy hadn't yet moved with the wheelbarrow. 'This job stinks Nic. You keep promising to take us overseas, too. You've taken us to South Australia, Tasmania and Victoria, but now you have us shovelling bird poo here up in Cairns.'

'Well, Sandy, this time, it's for real. The Border Police have called us in to deal with the nasties of Fauna smuggling. It isn't good at the moment. It's an animal breeding season, and these people don't care if the animals survive. They just want their money.

'That's horrible. So, it all leaves from here? Or is it just the snakes and lizards?'

'Yep, mainly from here, but it's anything small enough to get into a plastic tube or a suitcase.'

Rose grinned. 'But what about the budgie smugglers? I thought it was something one of our ex-prime Ministers wore at his local beach in summer.'

For more reading from the Nic Thorn and Associates series of scam-busting investigations look for these titles:

One tricked Phoney

Rose needed a +1, but not for the usual wedding/party. She was going to a funeral and needed a quiet, unassuming type. The best option was to use her dating site, but when Nic Thorn arrived, he was anything but a wallflower. He coerces them into his madcap investigations of scams, frauds, and misunderstandings. These modern-day adventures lead them from one lively caper to another, involving portrait provenance, invoice inaccuracy, and a recycler's relapse, on their travels from Brisbane, Adelaide, to the SA border.

Two hurtled Gloves

Welcome back to Nic's world of diversions and distractions, which begins on a golden beach in Port Douglas, tracks down to Tasmania, and up to the banks of Brisbane. Nic has to investigate a wedded miss, the misguided pretence of Tiger tracking, and some banking blasphemy. Rose was to be a bride again, but this time, it didn't exactly go off without a hitch, either. Then, they move on to another tale, this one tracking down the elusive and believed to be extinct Thylacine. Sandy loses her identity, and Nic introduces them to the benign world of banking, but there is much more involved when the loan arranger is unmasked as a fraud.

Four brooding Birds

The Australian Department of Agriculture often deals with sneaks and adders, and this time, Nic and the team are brought in to investigate reptile smuggling. Lizards have been discovered stuffed into a women's singlet, and her accomplice is caught with his jocks of frogs, but of course, they deny any knowledge of how they got in there. Then the team tries to drink from the sweet success of wines, but this just turns out to be someone who can't stop whining about how he has to keep everything bottled up inside and to complete their subsequent investigation, they have to look into genuine budgie smugglers.

Five mouldy Bins

This is the 5th novel in the Nic Thorn Caper series. It's Christmas in July, and the Department of Health in Brisbane is concerned that someone may be stuffing their mattress with ill-gotten gains, so Nic and the team bring it to a head – reindeer style. Meanwhile, Sandy and Rose meet up with their 'friend' Dimond, who keeps handing over her hard-earned money (she tells them that anyway) to lease a new rental property for her husband and family as it turns out the Real Estate Agent knows how to manage to take the deposit too, but only ever in cash. The team gets involved in a diamond scam. The resolution could be clear cut, but getting stranded in Dubai on the way to South Africa was never in the plan.

Six Geezers Lying

This time, they are brought in for a crash course into a car crashing. Car insurance companies are being driven up the wall by bogus claims and 'accidents', so it's time someone gives the scammers a crash course on stopping. Then, one of the national restaurant chains puts together a competition so quickly that anyone can win, but what happens when the prizes are won even before the competition is finished? Someone is already claiming the winnings. Is it a competition if there are only winners? Rose's Father likes to think he knows about art, so the team gets involved in an art scam. Can he afford to have his reputation tarnished? Art is not always art, as it depends on your point of view, but fraud is always a fraud.

Seven hapless Hoops

Organisations keep looking to Nic Thorn and his Associates to sort stuff out. A person is missing, a car is missing, and it's a lot of horsing around for Nic and his team. This time, one of his old friends calls upon him to locate his missing wife; whilst this is not generally within the scope of what they do, it is too close to home for Nic not to be in the right place to investigate. Meantime, a car vanishes without a trace, and a horse race is gathering pace, but will they be too late to save face?

AUTHOR'S BIOGRAPHY

The author is a former long-term banker by profession and worked within the Bank's Credit Card Fraud Team, where he obtained a Private Investigators License. The author resides between Adelaide, South Australia, and the Sunshine Coast, Queensland. He has been fortunate to have visited many places in Australia and includes them in these stories.

In November 2022, the author won an award from Wakefield Press, Adelaide for his short story: 'Car on a Hill'.